A Door of Hope

# Summerwind Books

A Door of Hope
Inside the Privet Hedge

# NEVA COYLE

# A Door of Hope

**BETHANY HOUSE PUBLISHERS**
Minneapolis, Minnesota 55438

Copyright © 1995
Neva Coyle

Published by Bethany House Publishers
A Ministry of Bethany Fellowship, Inc.
11300 Hampshire Avenue South
Minneapolis, Minnesota 55438

Printed in the United States of America.

---

**Library of Congress Cataloging-in-Publication Data**

Coyle, Neva.
    A door of hope / Neva Coyle.
       p.  cm. — (Summerwind)

    I. Title.  II. Series: Coyle, Neva. Summerwind.
PS3553.0957D6     1995
813'.54—dc20                                 95–485
ISBN 1–55661–475–6                      CIP

To Mom and Dad

NEVA COYLE is founder and author of the Overeaters Victorious Christian weight management concepts found in her bestselling books *The All-New Free to Be Thin* and *The All-New Free to Be Thin Lifestyle Plan*. She is the President of Neva Coyle Ministries and recently her prolific writing career and speaking ministry has been enhanced with the addition of writing fiction. As well as being a gifted motivational speaker/teacher, Neva is actively involved in the ministries of her local church. Neva and her husband live in California.

Requests for materials should go to:

P.O. Box 1638
Oakhurst, CA 93644

# Prologue

A hush fell across the crowd gathered in Summer-wind's outdoor community amphitheater for the Class of 1957's graduation exercises. The newest, and youngest, pastor of the community had opened the ceremony by delivering a stirring invocation. Finally, the last of the more than three hundred graduates received their diplomas. Now the class stood in the traditional silence as the carillon in the church four blocks away played the alma mater in their honor.

The graduates, full of promise and hope, were eager to get the momentous ceremony over with and move on with their lives. Many were looking forward to college; others were heading out into the work force. All were visibly excited and happy—except for one.

Karissa Hill stood in the fourth row, six places from the end. She, too, lowered her head in silent reverence as her tears fell unchecked on the front of her white graduation robe. Her blue and white tassel rustled slightly in the light breeze. She didn't hear the notes of the cherished song chiming through the evening in honor of the class of '57. She was lost in her own thoughts of the future—a future already decided, already sealed.

Karissa was going to have to find a way to tell her parents she wasn't going to college after all. To tell them she was not only married—married to Michael

Allen Andrews—but that she was going to have his baby. She closed her eyes in an effort to shut out her fear and pain. The night she and Michael eloped, they had agreed to keep their marriage a secret until graduation. Last night he had even tried to convince her to wait until the end of the summer. But by then she'd be nearly five months into her pregnancy. She was already beginning to notice the changes in her body—how did he think she could hide this much longer? She had watched her own mother go through this too many times not to know better. The nausea she felt each morning was getting worse, too, and harder to hide.

She didn't understand his reasons. They loved each other—didn't they? She couldn't keep the news of their marriage and her pregnancy trapped within her much longer. She had to find a way to tell someone.

Michael would be furious; Karissa knew that for sure. He might even hit her again. But if her parents knew they were married and expecting a baby, maybe then the beatings would stop.

Suddenly cheers erupted from her classmates as they threw their graduation caps high into the air. Karissa removed her cap, but she didn't throw it. Clutching it tightly against her slender body, she made the decision. As soon as she could get her mother alone, she would tell her. She knew Kate Hill would understand. But her father? Well, Gerald Hill's reaction would be . . . Karissa didn't let her thoughts wander further.

The graduates filed off the platform into the arms of waiting families and friends. Karissa hugged her mother while her father stood a little way off. She looked around for Michael. He said he'd be here.

After returning her cap and gown, Karissa walked obediently between her parents back to the family car. Other graduates chattered happily around her, making their last-minute plans for parties. She would go home with her parents. Michael said if he didn't see her at graduation, he'd see her later at her house.

Fighting back tears of disappointment, she waited until half past midnight before she climbed the stairs to her room. Covering her head with her pillow, Karissa Kathleen Hill Andrews cried herself to sleep— again.

# One

Karissa stumbled toward the incessant knocking at the front door of her small two-bedroom house. With each step, sharp pains from her throbbing, swollen ankle shot through her leg and foot.

She glanced toward the gold-toned sunburst clock centered above the small fireplace mantel in the living room. Barely able to read the time in the darkened room, she continued limping toward the door.

"Two-thirty," she muttered to herself, "and too drunk to get his key in the lock."

Karissa flung open the front door, about to lash out at her husband.

"Is Mrs. Andrews home?" a dark-haired police officer asked, removing his hat.

"What?" Startled, Karissa pulled her bathrobe more tightly about her.

"Miss, I'm Officer Mendez and this is my partner, Officer Hendricks. May we come in?"

Stepping away from the door, Karissa put too much weight on her twisted ankle and, with a small cry, fell toward the overstuffed chair beside the doorway.

"Here, let me help you," Mendez offered.

"Thank you." Karissa gingerly made her way around the chair and sat down heavily.

"You alone here, miss?"

"For now. My husband is out with his friends. He should be back any minute. I thought it was him when you came . . ." Karissa's voice trailed off as she caught the knowing glances exchanged between the police officers.

"Your husband?"

"Yes . . . Michael." Karissa's heart pounded wildly, and her head throbbed.

"Can we turn on a light?" Hendricks found the switch and illuminated the room.

"There's been an accident, uh . . . Mrs. Andrews," Mendez began. "Is there someone who can come stay with you tonight? Your parents maybe, or a neighbor?"

"Yeah, my parents live here in town, over on Sonora Street."

"Could we call them?"

"They don't have a phone." Karissa waited for more information about Michael. What kind of accident? Drunk driving? Had he injured someone? Or worse?

"How can we reach your—"

"What kind of accident?" Karissa interrupted. "Is Michael all right? What's this got to do with my parents?"

"We just don't think you should be alone right now, Mrs. Andrews. Do you have a phone?"

"Yes, in there," said Karissa, pointing toward the kitchen, "but I told you, they don't have a phone."

Hendricks moved toward the kitchen and called back, "What's their address?"

"Two-fifty Sonora." Karissa strained to catch the officer's voice as he ordered the dispatcher to send a squad car to her parents' house.

"Please, is this about Michael?" She turned back to the dark-haired officer, frustration tinging her voice.

Mendez squatted down in front of her and looked gently into her eyes. Karissa knew she could not hide the fact that she'd spent the last several hours crying. She could feel the burning of her still-swollen eyes and the aching throb of her bruised cheekbone. She averted her eyes, ashamed to have anyone see her like this.

Officer Mendez took ahold of her hands and carefully turned them to examine the bruises above her wrists. "Did your husband do this to you?"

Shrugging, Karissa searched the officer's kind face. "What about the accident? Is Michael all right?"

Hendricks came into the room and nodded. Mendez began, "Michael has been . . ." He glanced toward his partner, then back to Karissa. "There's no easy way to tell you this, Mrs. Andrews. Michael is dead."

Karissa's heart stopped pounding—it felt as if it had stopped altogether. Her head throbbed, refusing the news.

"What?" She could barely speak above a whisper.

"He drowned." Hendricks pulled up the small wooden rocker Karissa kept beside the table at the front window.

"Drowned? How? . . . I don't understand."

"He and some of his friends were skinny-dipping at the YMCA. They'd broken in after hours and were swimming in the dark. Michael must have slipped and fell, or maybe dived into the shallow end. We're not sure. In any case, he was knocked out, and in the dark his friends didn't realize he was underwater until Jimmy Hernandez stumbled over him and pulled him out. By then it was too late."

Stunned, Karissa stared at the two officers facing her. She put her hand across her mouth and sat motionless for a few moments, then bolted to the kitchen sink and began to vomit uncontrollably.

Mendez quickly came to her side and put his arm around her waist and his hand across her forehead. Her whole body shook and retched. Finally, spent and shaky, she leaned into the kind officer and began to cry—quietly at first, then in deep convulsing sobs.

"Here . . ." Mendez tried awkwardly to comfort her. "Why don't you sit down again?" He led her to a chair by the small kitchen table and helped her down. She winced in pain as his hand touched more bruises on her arm.

"Is there anywhere you're not bruised?" he asked, the anger in his voice barely suppressed.

Karissa shrugged between sobs.

"Did Michael do this to you?"

"We had a fight last night."

"An uneven match, I'd say."

They both turned at the sound of a knock and a woman's voice at the front door. "Hello? Kassy? Is everything all right?"

Officer Hendricks went to open the door. "Are you Mrs. Andrews' mother?" he asked the woman.

"No . . . I'm Mathilda Sloan, Kassy's next-door neighbor. I saw your car out front and wondered if I might be useful here. If not, I can . . ."

"Have her come in, Hendricks," Mendez called to his partner from the kitchen. "Mrs. Andrews here could use a friendly face."

"Kassy, my dear"—Mattie moved quickly to Karissa's side—"what's happened?"

"Oh, Mattie . . . Michael's dead!"

"What?" Mattie's voice rose with surprise and shock.

"I'm afraid it's true," Mendez offered. "He drowned swimming with some friends at the Y."

"When did this happen?"

"Just past one."

"This morning?"

Mendez nodded. Mattie turned to Karissa and smoothed back her hair. Karissa winced as Mattie's fingers brushed yet another bruise on her temple.

Exchanging a knowing glance with Mendez, Mattie reached for Karissa's hands and pushed the sleeves of her robe up above her wrists.

"Are you hurt anywhere else?" Mattie asked quietly, her voice trembling.

"My ankle."

"Let's see." Mattie bent over to have a look. "Pretty swollen. Think you should have a doctor look at it?"

"No." Karissa's stomach wrenched with fear. "Please, no. I'll be all right." She reached toward the older woman. "Mattie, Michael's dead. I can't believe it. Oh, Mattie, what am I going to do?"

Mattie straightened up and stood beside Karissa. Pulling the girl gently to her bosom, Mattie began to soothe her and lightly stroke her hair. "Shhh now, my love. You don't have to do anything right now.

"Has someone contacted her parents?" Mattie asked.

Mendez nodded.

"And Michael's?"

He nodded again.

"Is my mother coming over?" Karissa asked, anxiety in her voice.

"We sent someone to tell your parents."

Mattie stayed with Karissa in the kitchen while the two officers stepped outside.

"What a jerk!" Mendez found his anger fighting for expression as he paced back and forth on the small front stoop. "I'm sorry, but I can't help feeling he got what he deserved. Did you see that shiner she's got?"

"It'll be worse by morning," Hendricks said.

"And in full bloom by the funeral. There'll be no hiding what went on here before he went out for his midnight swim." He continued to pace. "She's no older than my own daughter Patsy. I just wanted to hold her and tell her everything'll be okay."

Hendricks gave a knowing nod.

"Sometimes I hate this job." Mendez stopped his pacing and stared at the deserted street, fighting to control his anger at the now-deceased Michael Andrews.

"Hey, how're those Yanks lookin' for the pennant?" Hendricks asked in an obvious attempt to take Mendez's mind off the young woman inside. "Ol' Casey Stengel can't afford any losses. He's probably got this year and maybe another. Gettin' old, I'd say."

"He'll do all right." Mendez was thankful for the diversion. "Those Yanks'll come through."

"Bettin' on them this year for the Series?"

"I'm not a bettin' man, Hendricks, you know that. Anyway, Milwaukee's lookin' mighty strong this year. That young Hank Aaron is something. He'll be a great hitter, you watch."

"Thought you to be a Yanks fan through and through, Mendez."

"Wonder what could be keeping her mother? What's it been? Thirty, forty minutes?" Mendez was pacing again.

"You see *Bridge on the River Kwai* yet?" Hendricks went on. "Won three Oscars, you know. Showin' at the drive-in again. You ought to take the wife and go on out this weekend," Hendricks said, trying to calm his partner.

"Yeah, sure."

"Hey, you think Nixon will run for President? Ike's been pretty good to him. Bein' VP may be just the setup he needs." Mendez shot his partner a frustrated look. Hendricks dropped the subject. It was no use.

"I can't understand how someone could do that to her." Mendez nodded toward the house. "How could her parents stand by and see her mixed up with someone like this, anyway?" He checked his watch. "Can't figure what's keepin' her parents. If that'd been one of my kids, I would've been here half an hour ago."

————

Across town at two-fifty Sonora, Kathleen Hill pleaded with her husband. "I have to go to her, Gerry. She's my daughter, for heaven's sake."

"Leave heaven out of this!" Gerald warned. "I told her he was no good. I knew this marriage would end in disaster. She made her bed—let her lie in it!"

"I'm going to her!" Kate had never opposed or disobeyed her husband before now. "Give me the keys!"

"You crazy? Didn't you hear me? You're going nowhere. You've got family that needs you here. The kids will be up in a couple of hours. Who'll take care of them?"

"You're their father! You do it!"

Kate's face stung from Gerald's sudden slap. She grabbed her cheek, then straightened her shoulders. She took a deep breath and a quiet calm rose within her.

"I'm sorry, Kate." Gerald stood trembling before her, his eyes filled with both anger and regret.

She wouldn't give him the satisfaction of acknowledging his apology—not this time, not ever again. Kate was seeing her husband clearly for the first time. *He's just like his father—headstrong and stubborn—and he's never going to change!*

With renewed resolve, Kate dressed quickly and reached for her sweater as she left the room without a backward glance.

"Kate, come back here!" Gerald yelled after her. "Don't leave me!"

"I'm going to Karissa! Even if I have to walk!"

"But the kids!"

"*You* take care of things here until I get back." Kate had never called Gerald's bluff before. She suddenly felt exhilarated and free.

"But I can't handle the kids alone!" Gerald's voice held a tinge of pout as well as anger now. "You're their mother—they need you! I'm no baby-sitter!"

Kate stopped and discovered new strength rising in her, a strength she'd never felt before.

"Listen to you! All you have to do is fix a simple breakfast, help them get off to school, and get Sandy's mother to watch Edie and the baby. You can't do that? You want Karissa to face the death of her husband alone, arrange a funeral alone, and face Michael's parents alone, but you can't put a simple box of Cheerios on the table and pour the milk?" Kate was shocked by her own words and the edge of shame they carried. She saw Gerald back away from her unexpected rage.

"I'll call Margie to let you know when I'll be back." Kate stepped out into the night and quietly closed the door behind her. Despite all the yelling, the baby was still asleep. She certainly didn't want to wake her now. Gerald would need somewhere to focus his anger, and she didn't want it to be on the baby.

"Give you a lift?" Kate was surprised to find Ned waiting in his car at the curb. "We heard the commotion, saw your lights. Margie sent me to investigate. I overheard . . . I'm sorry. Thought you might need a ride."

Kate glanced toward the neighbors' house. Margie was standing on the porch waving as her husband blinked the headlights at her.

"Don't worry. Margie will go over and help get the kids off to school. She'll take the baby, too. Sandy's getting up, and when I get back, she'll be waiting to see if it's a good idea for her to go over to Kassy's, too."

Kate smiled gratefully at her kind neighbor. If it hadn't been for Sandy's friendship with Karissa—

well, she was thankful for more than one interrupting knock at the back door when Gerry's temper flared. Sandy had been a pipeline of information to her parents, and several times Margie or Ned had saved Kate from Gerry's outbursts.

"Gerry just doesn't understand." Kate tried to convince herself more than Ned. "He is still so hurt that Kassy is married to Michael."

"She's not anymore."

"Pardon me?" Kate didn't understand Ned's comment.

"She's not married anymore. Not to Michael, not to anyone."

"You're right." Kate's thoughts raced toward her eldest daughter. "I wonder what she'll do now?"

"Do?"

"Gerry will never let her come home. He's made that clear more than once."

"Maybe he'll change his mind."

"Gerry?" Kate's laugh was cutting. "No, he won't change his mind. It's a matter of pride now."

"But what . . ."

"She'll have to find her way on her own, I guess. I'm sure there must be some insurance or something. His parents are quite well off, you know. Maybe they'll help her." Kate's mind wandered back over the past few months. Remembering the look of anguish on Phyllis Andrews' face when Michael and Karissa announced they had eloped the night of the Jubilee prom last January, Kate wrapped her arms tightly around herself. "Michael's mother was just as upset by the marriage as Gerry was."

"I remember." Ned turned onto Karissa's street.

"The police are still here," Kate observed, "but I don't see the Andrewses' car. Nor Michael's." Kate glanced through the windshield and saw wisps of pink streaking across the somber sky. "What time is it, Ned?"

"Four-thirty, maybe a quarter to five. Want me to go in with you?"

"Would you? Thanks."

"It's going to be a long day, Kate. Ready?"

"I'm about as ready for this as I am another baby, Ned." She reached for the door handle, then turned back to her neighbor. "But just like then, I'll have to face it and do what I have to do."

Ned gave her an understanding pat on the arm. "I know you will, Kate. And we'll be here for you."

Together, they mounted the steps of the small house. As she opened the door the sight of her daughter brought tears of shame to Kate's eyes. He had beaten her . . . again.

"Mama." Karissa slowly tried to stand to greet her mother, but sat back down, exhaustion and pain etching her features.

"Kassy!" Kate suppressed the grateful feeling that Michael would never be able to touch her daughter again. She pushed away the thought that even though Kassy didn't know it yet, her life would be better now. Kneeling in front of Karissa, Kate tenderly enclosed her daughter in her arms.

Karissa buried her face in her mother's warm neck, and once again, her slight young body heaved with sobs.

# Two

"Are there many more like this?" Kate asked Karissa as she helped her change into a clean nightgown.

"I don't really know, Mama." Embarrassed, Karissa grabbed for the gown in her mother's hands.

"Turn around, Kassy. I'm your mother, for heaven's sake. Let me see your back."

Karissa turned slowly. Low on her back, a bright blue bruise was only half-visible above the elastic on her panties. Kate gasped in shock. Karissa tried to turn back. "No, Karissa, I want to see the whole thing."

Kate gently tugged Karissa's underwear away from the bruise and caught her breath. "He really did it to you this time, didn't he?"

Karissa's eyes spilled tears down her cheeks and onto her bare chest, which she covered with her arms. Kate bent to examine her daughter's marked thighs and noticed some of the bruises there were turning green.

Taking her daughter tenderly by the shoulders, she turned Karissa toward her. "You're too thin, Kassy."

"Mama, please." Karissa grabbed for the clean gown again. "Can I have my nightie now?"

While Kate was helping lower the gown over Karissa's head, she glanced down at her daughter's slightly bulging tummy.

"Karissa! Are you pregnant?"

Karissa turned away from her mother, pulled her nightgown down into place, and hugged herself. She walked toward the window and stared. The window shade was down, but she wasn't looking out the window. She was looking, as she had done so many other times, into the future—into nothing. Nothing, that is, until she knew she was going to have a baby.

Michael had been enraged yesterday when she'd tried to talk about the baby. Yesterday? It felt like a week or even a month ago, but it was only last night that Michael had screamed at her again for being so careless.

*"Don't you know how to take care of yourself? You aren't the woman I married! You're sick all the time now 'cause of that stupid baby!"* She could still hear his angry voice just before his knuckles slammed across her cheek and sent her reeling backward onto the kitchen table.

"Don't you know how to take care of yourself?" Kate asked.

Her mother's question jolted Karissa back to the present. "That's exactly what Michael said. . . ." Karissa's voice cracked and her eyes once again spilled her never-ending reservoir of tears.

"Oh, honey, I didn't mean—"

"Most of the time, yes. But when Michael . . . I mean sometimes he didn't give me time. . . . He was so . . . you know, in a hurry."

"And you?"

"What about me?"

"Were you in a hurry too?"

"Mama . . . please. I don't want to talk about this."

"I want to know it all, Karissa." Kate guided her daughter to sit on the bed beside her, wrapping her arm around her shoulder.

"It's just that—" Karissa didn't know how to talk

about such things with her mother. "Sometimes, you know, well, he said women needed persuasion. It was too much work and . . . well, Michael said that force was just as good." Karissa twisted her nightgown in her hands and spoke barely above a whisper. "I tried, Mama. I tried to be a good wife. I don't think Michael was happy with me. . . ." Her voice gave way to quiet sobs.

Kate took hold of Karissa's shoulders again and turned her daughter to face her directly. "Listen to yourself, Kassy. You have no reason to blame yourself. Michael beat you and he raped you. . . . *You* are not to blame for his unhappiness."

Kate was appalled at the anger she felt rising toward her dead son-in-law. "I'm trying very hard not to be thankful that he's gone."

"Mama!"

"God forgive me, Karissa." Kate stood and turned to help Karissa into bed. "You need some rest. I have some pills in my purse. They'll help you sleep."

"Will it hurt the baby?"

"If that little baby can survive its father's beatings, one little pill isn't going to hurt him or her a bit."

"Let me try without it first, okay?"

"Have you heard from the Andrewses?" Kate pulled up the covers and tucked them in around her daughter.

"No, not yet. I will, though."

"Try to sleep, baby." Kate leaned over and kissed Karissa's forehead.

"Mama?"

"Yes."

"You won't leave me, will you, Mama?"

"No, Kassy, I won't leave. Margie is looking out for the kids."

"What about Daddy?"

"Daddy is going to have to take care of himself for a few days."

"But won't he be mad?"

"Probably. Don't you worry. . . ." Kate's tone was firm and resolute. "I can take care of your daddy."

Karissa's eyes closed, and Kate sat down in a small wing chair in the corner. She leaned her head back against the fine brocade upholstery. In all the years she had been married, she had never had a room as lovely as this. Phyllis Andrews' taste was displayed everywhere.

Once she had accepted the marriage, Karissa's mother-in-law had thrown herself into helping Michael plan and decorate his first home. Karissa didn't know anything about keeping a home, other than taking care of her younger brothers and sisters and cooking and cleaning all day on Saturdays.

Kate noticed her daughter's breathing deepen, become even, except for the occasional sob that caught Kate's heart off guard. She looked so small lying there in the oversized bed. Kate turned her mind from the cruelty, even brutality, that Karissa had endured there.

Quietly, Kate stood and wandered over to the mirrored closet doors. She slid the door open and glanced over the clothes hanging inside. Michael's plentiful supply of sweaters, jackets, pants, and shirts took up most of the space. Karissa's few clothes were hung neatly at the other end.

The top shelves were lined with shoe boxes bearing the most expensive brand names in men's shoes. Karissa's sandals were on the floor beneath her jeans and one sundress. Her high school letter sweater hung covered with plastic. Kate couldn't recall seeing Karissa wearing it after graduation. But then, this was only September.

Karissa should be planning what classes to take

at the community college, what she would wear, and how she and Sandy would manage to get there and back each day. Instead, Karissa Kathleen Hill Andrews would be planning a funeral. And facing life with a baby and no husband.

Kate looked at her sleeping daughter once again and stepped quietly out of the room. She had never been alone in Karissa's home before. An hour at a time, at the very most, was all she could manage to get away from her own house and her younger children.

She walked toward the second bedroom and looked briefly inside. The room was not yet finished. Wallpaper rolls lay on the floor, and a new daybed, still covered in plastic, stood to one side. The single window was bare except for a simple shade. The smell of varnish lingered on the refinished woodwork.

*"They'll spoil those kids!"* Gerald had objected when Phyllis and Mark Andrews put up the money for a generous down payment on the house. *"That boy will never learn to be a man if his mommy keeps buying them things! Let him work for his living, like the rest of us."* Kate knew Gerald was right, but his tone and attitude were wrong. Gerald Hill was jealous of his own daughter's home and furnishings.

Kate walked into the small, bright kitchen and noticed with pride how clean and perfect Karissa kept everything. Opening the cupboard, she took a bright-patterned cup and saucer from the shelf. Turning to the stove, she set the teakettle in place and left the lid up so it wouldn't whistle and wake Karissa when it reached boiling. She opened a few cupboard doors before she spotted tea bags inside a translucent white plastic container.

Carrying her cup of tea into the living room, she glanced at the sunburst clock over the mantel. Seven-thirty. She could hear the routine sounds of morning in the neighborhood. She started as the paper plunked against the screen door. Eventually the milkman delivered two quarts of milk at the back door and knocked loudly before he turned and hurried on his way.

Life for Karissa had drastically changed in less than twelve hours, yet the routine of the neighborhood was unchanged. Kate felt as if she were watching it all on a movie screen. She settled into a comfortable armchair and sipped her hot tea.

The sound of tires on loose gravel in the driveway caught her attention, but she didn't get up to see who it was until she heard the light rapping on the back door.

"Mr. Andrews. Please, come in." Kate stepped aside and motioned for the haggard-looking man to enter. She noticed the expensive cut of his suit and how his tie hung loosely at his neck. His starched white shirt was open at the collar, and though he was clean-shaven, she knew he had been up all night.

"I brought Michael's car." He could barely speak. "How's Kassy?"

"Sleeping."

"Good . . ." Mark sighed.

"I'm having a cup of tea—the water's still hot. Would you like a cup? Or perhaps coffee?"

"Thank you." Mark sunk into a kitchen chair and slumped slightly forward. "I'd like that very much."

"Have you eaten?"

"No, I don't think I could . . ."

"I'll fix you something. Let me see."

"Please don't. I don't want you to bother. I'm not sure I could swallow it."

"You're in for a very long day, Mr. Andrews. Let me just put in some toast. If you don't want it, then don't eat it. But it will make me feel better if I can fix it, okay?"

"Mark."

"Pardon me?"

"Call me Mark. Okay, I'll try to eat some toast."

"You must know, Mr. Andrews—Mark—how sorry I am about your son." Kate groped for the right words.

"You don't have to say anything, Mrs. Hill."

"Kate."

"Kate." Mark paused. "I loved my son, that's true. But we were never close. Strange as it sounds, I guess I feel almost as badly for what we never had. When the police came last night, Phyllis became hysterical. We called the doctor. He came and gave her a shot. Put her right out. We don't expect her to wake up until sometime this afternoon. Maria, our housekeeper, is with her now."

Kate noticed the faraway look on Mark's face—numbness, she guessed.

"How is Karissa doing?" Mark asked.

"She's coping. She slept without too much trouble. I offered her some of my nerve pills, but she didn't want to . . ." Kate didn't finish; she didn't know if Mark knew about the baby. She thought of Phyllis up on "the hill," in her big house in her satin-covered bed, being watched over by her housekeeper.

She watched Mark take a bite of his toast and wondered if he could even taste it.

"I dread her waking up," Mark said. "She's having a very hard time with this."

Kate swallowed a cryptic remark.

"I'm more worried about Karissa than Phyllis, though." Mark's comment took Kate by surprise. "Are you shocked?"

"A little, yes."

"I'm not unaware that Karissa got the rotten end of the deal when she married my son."

Kate carefully replaced her cup on the matching

saucer. "Really? Are you sure?"

"Quite." Mark played with the toast crumbs on the table. Kate saw him squash them one by one with his middle finger for a moment before she stood to find a dishrag to wipe them up. Mark's hand on her arm restrained her before she could move away from the table.

"Please, sit down. Don't fuss. I can't stand any more fussing."

Kate sat and looked directly into the pain in Mark's eyes.

"I've never gotten to know you very well, Kate. Gerald either. I'm sorry about that. You seem like the kind of people I'd like to know."

Kate sipped her tea, even though it was almost cold.

"You probably find that hard to believe."

"Well, you've hardly gone out of your way to—"

"I *am* sorry. . . ."

"This isn't a good time to talk about that now, Mark. Michael and Karissa are what's important now."

"Only Karissa, Kate. Thank God we still have Karissa."

Kate marveled at his words. Karissa's own father never spoke of her so affectionately. Kate wondered if she should tell Mark about the baby, when she heard Karissa in the bathroom throwing up.

"My God!" Mark said. "Is she sick?"

"Not really." Kate hoped he'd catch on.

Mark's eyes widened. He stood and ran his hand through his hair and thrust the other deep in his pants pocket. He turned his back on Kate and looked out the small kitchen door window. He stood quietly until the sounds in the bathroom stopped and they heard Karissa return to her room. Then he turned back to Kate.

"Whatever we do, please, listen to me—make sure she doesn't tell Phyllis."

"Oh?"

"Please, Kate. Do this—not for me, but for Karissa and for the baby. Let's get through the next few weeks without Phyllis knowing . . ." He looked pleadingly at Kate. "It's not Phyllis I'm thinking of—it's Kassy."

"All right, if you think it's necessary. I'll do what I can."

"I want to see Karissa. Do you think she'd see me? It's important. You know, funeral, burial, and all that." Mark looked apologetic.

"Please, Mark, she knows this is coming. But you need to know something first. She doesn't look too . . . well, I don't know quite how to tell you this. . . ."

"Mama?" Karissa called from the hall.

"Mark, Michael wasn't too happy about the baby. He—"

"You in here?" Karissa slowly opened the door to the kitchen.

"Kassy?" Mark's face registered shock and pain.

"Oh, Mark." Karissa limped across the room and into her father-in-law's embrace. "I'm so sorry about Michael. I woke up and for a moment I didn't believe it. I looked out the back window and saw his car out by the garage and thought I'd had a bad dream."

Mark's eyes filled with tears and he looked across the room to catch Kate's glance. "Karissa, don't worry, everything will be all right."

"But Michael's never coming back." Karissa sobbed against Mark's chest.

"Shh. Hush now." Mark tried to soothe Karissa, then pulled himself from her clasp and held her at arm's length. "What happened to you, Kassy? Did Michael do this to you?"

She didn't need to answer. Pulling her to him, he

tenderly wrapped his arms around her. Mark buried his face in Karissa's fine blond hair before he gave voice to the sobs choking him. "It won't happen again, Karissa," he said finally. "Thank God, it won't happen again."

# Three

Standing beside Michael's casket under the bright blue and white striped canopy, Karissa was grateful for the green matting discreetly covering the gaping hole below. The afternoon September sun was warm and Karissa felt tired. She had been spared making any of the final decisions or even visiting the funeral home until Michael's body was presented for viewing.

She had only asked two things. First, for the funeral to begin at one o'clock in the afternoon. She wanted to be safely past any chance of morning sickness. Her mother had expressed concern that she was still having problems with that, being nearly five months along. Karissa couldn't take the chance of Phyllis finding out about the baby, not just yet. She also asked that the casket remain closed during the service. The funeral director agreed. He neglected, however, to give closed-casket instructions to his assistants, and at the end of the service Karissa had been stunned when she had to pass by the open box one more time on the way from the chapel.

She had gathered her courage to approach the open casket, and Mark had stood at her elbow as she silently stared at the expressionless face of her young husband. She remembered how angry he used to look when he was in one of his moods or had been drinking.

Now she stood surrounded by family and friends at the graveside. Kate stood to Karissa's left, her arm linked through her daughter's. Gerald was noticeably absent. Karissa glanced occasionally toward the cemetery gate, hoping that he might still show up. Mark Andrews stood to her right, and on his other side was Phyllis, who was tranquilized into a barely conscious state. Even so, Phyllis wore the latest in fashion—a black silk suit, a matching veiled hat, and gloves. Her stockings, too, were black, and her low pumps sleek and expensive.

Karissa wore a simple navy blue linen shirtwaist-style dress and navy gloves. Grateful for the elastic at the waist and the bit of space left to poke another hole in the end of the belt, she held her clutch purse self-consciously across her slightly rounded stomach and hoped no one would notice her condition. She had let her mother persuade her to cover her head with a tricornered navy lace scarf during the service, but she let it fall to her shoulders in the breeze at the cemetery.

Mark edged Karissa, Kate, and Phyllis toward the row of folding chairs reserved for the family members.

Karissa knew the minister was speaking, trying to console the mourning family. But she was drawn to the tall, slender cypress bushes lining the wrought-iron fence. She wondered if the view would be blocked by the bushes, in case her father did arrive after all. Then she sighed and said aloud, "I guess it doesn't really matter, does it?"

"Karissa?" Mark whispered.

"Oh, nothing," she responded flatly.

Karissa had moved through the last few days grateful for her mother's company and her friend Sandy's gentle encouragement. Mark had come to see her several times each day to talk over funeral arrangements and details with her. Phyllis stayed in her bed, drugged. Karissa was grateful that she hadn't had to deal with her overbearing mother-in-law before today. Safe within the company of her socialite friends, Phyllis would be the perfect picture of the adoring, grieving mother.

"Ashes to ashes . . ." Karissa barely heard the minister's traditional words, "and dust to dust . . ."

A younger man stepped forward to stand next to the more formal-looking minister.

"Just as we are about to commit the body of Michael Andrews back into the soil from which God created man, we must also commit ourselves to life."

Karissa felt she should know this young minister, but she couldn't place him. She glanced at Mark, who smiled slightly in her direction and patted her hand reassuringly. She noticed Phyllis glaring angrily at her husband.

"There is no sorrow that God cannot heal. No prayer of loneliness He cannot hear. There is no regret He cannot touch and no sin He cannot forgive."

Phyllis shifted unsteadily in the folding chair. Mark reached to steady her, and she shrugged away from his touch.

"I leave you with a passage of Scripture from the book of Hosea, chapter two, verses fourteen and fifteen." The young man read from a white card: " 'I . . . will bring her into the wilderness, and speak comfortably unto her. And I will give her vineyards from thence, and the valley of Achor for a door of hope: and she shall sing there, as in the days of her youth. . . . ' Let us pray."

"Our Father God . . ."

Karissa stared openly at the young man who had stepped aside to let the older minister close the brief service with a prayer he read from a book. *Hope?* Of all the things she might have expected to hear about today, hope was not among them.

Back at the Andrewses' house, the afternoon was

filled with people coming and going. Relatives complained they only saw one another at weddings and funerals. Friends and neighbors formed little groups and exchanged local news. Kate was more comfortable helping serve the funeral guests, so she joined Maria, the Andrewses' housekeeper, in the kitchen every time she could find an excuse to do so.

"Beautiful service . . ." said an elderly woman.

"Call if there is anything I can do . . ." offered someone who looked familiar but whom Karissa couldn't remember.

When people finally began to leave, Karissa was exhausted.

"Karissa," Mark said, "I want you to meet James Henry. He's the pastor at River Place Community Church. He's been my friend for some time now."

Karissa looked up into the face of the young minister who had read from the white card at the cemetery.

He took her hand warmly. "Karissa? I'm sorry to meet you under such tragic circumstances."

Karissa nodded.

"I have written out the verses I read today, and I want you to have the card. You might want to read them for yourself later."

"Thank you," Karissa said, noticing the graceful handwriting on the card. "Thank you very much. I appreciate this."

"If you ever need anything . . . if you need to talk or if you want someone to pray with you . . . anything at all . . . please don't hesitate to call. My name and number are on the other side."

"Thank you, Reverend—"

"Jim, just Jim."

"Shallow words of comfort, hollow words of hope," Phyllis muttered loudly to a nearby friend. "What does he know of sorrow?"

"May I go home now, Mark?" Karissa asked. "I'm very tired."

"Of course. Let's get your mother."

"She's probably in the kitchen," Sandy offered from behind Karissa. "I'll get her."

"Are you feeling all right, Kassy?" Mark asked.

"Just tired. And my ankle hurts."

Mark winced at her remark. His own pain in these tragic circumstances was evident in every line and furrow of his face. "Have you seen a doctor yet?"

"Doctor?" Phyllis's strident voice erupted from the crowd.

"Yes, Karissa here has a . . . a . . ."

"A sprained ankle. I turned it the other night."

"Oh?" Phyllis raised an eyebrow.

"I tend to be a bit clumsy, Mrs. Andrews."

"So I've heard. Maybe you should have it X-rayed. Do you even have a doctor?"

"It'll be fine. I just need to put ice on it and get off my feet."

Karissa excused herself suddenly as she spotted her mother with Sandy's parents. She was grateful for the chance to get away from her mother-in-law's questions. The small entourage walked quickly to Ned and Margie's car. Ned removed the funeral tag from beneath the windshield wiper blade.

"May I have that?" Karissa asked.

"Sure." Ned handed the small red tag to her and she stuck it in her purse, along with the white card from Jim Henry.

———

"Mama?" Karissa turned to her mother once she was settled in her own bed. "Can you stay with me one more night?"

"Of course, Kassy. Aunt Helen came down last night and said she'd stay with the family for a day or two so I could be with you."

"I can't go home, Mama."

"I know, sweetheart."

"I don't know what I'm going to do." Karissa closed her eyes against the uncertainty of her future.

"It's time to rest now, honey. We'll talk about this tomorrow. Okay?"

"Mama, will you sleep here with me?"

"If you want me to."

"Thanks."

Kate watched her oldest daughter—a widow not yet twenty years old and carrying a child of her own—snuggle deep into her pillow. Kate changed quickly into her nightgown and slipped between the covers next to Karissa. Putting out her arms, she gathered her daughter close to her.

Kate longed for the comfort of her husband's arms as she lay holding Kassy. There were the good times, of course. She loved Gerry more than her very life. Every time he had one of his "outbursts," she forgave him. What else could she do? She'd love him until she drew her last breath; that she knew for sure. But she hoped, sooner or later, he'd change. If not. . . ? As much as she wanted the change to be voluntary, she knew he might never have to change unless change was forced. But for now, there was Kassy to think about. Kate kissed her daughter's forehead and stroked her long hair.

There was no way to protect Karissa, no way to even shelter her from the harsh realities she'd have to face, if not tomorrow, certainly the day after. Tonight, she could only hold her close as she had longed to do so many times before. But that was all in the past. What had Jim Henry said? A door of hope. She'd hold on to that thought for Karissa; she might even attempt to pray again. She'd begin with prayers for her daughter. She could do that much for Karissa.

"Thank you, heavenly Father," she whispered into Karissa's hair. "Thank you for these few days in which I could once again touch my baby." For the first time, Kate's own tears flowed freely into Karissa's soft honey blond hair. "Dear God, please help us face the days ahead . . . and help me face Gerry, once and for all."

# Four

"What day is it?" Karissa leaned sleepily against the kitchen doorway.

Kate looked away from the scene out the kitchen window to her daughter. "It's Wednesday."

"I didn't even know what day it was." Karissa turned suddenly and headed down the hallway toward the bathroom. "Excuse me," she called back as she rushed to accommodate her morning sickness.

Kate frowned. "It's only supposed to last a few weeks—a month or two at the most," she called after her.

"What's that?" Mark poked his head in the back door. "I saw you at the window. Is it too early? Should I come back later?"

"Please, come in." Kate moved to close the kitchen door and was able to shut out the sounds of sickness coming from the bathroom—almost.

"How long will this go on?" he asked.

"That's what worries me," Kate said. "As far as I can tell, it should have been over long ago. It usually only lasts a month or two. I don't know for sure how far along she is—four, maybe even five months."

"But she's so small—she's not even showing," Mark protested.

"I know," Kate said. "But we both know she's not had an easy time of it." Kate poured Mark a cup of coffee. "Black?"

"Thanks."

"Does Phyllis know?"

"Not yet."

"Are you going to tell her?"

"Not yet."

"Hmm." Kate nodded and sipped her own steaming cup. She put the teakettle on the back burner and found a tea bag before joining Mark at the table. They sat peacefully in silence, something neither of them quite knew how to handle but both enjoyed for the moment.

"I think I'm done." Karissa looked pale and drawn as she came and joined Kate and Mark at the table.

"I'm making you some tea. Here's a cracker. That should help settle things a bit. Tonight, put some on a small plate by your bed. Eat them before you get up. It helps."

Karissa nodded.

"Are you going to be here alone, Karissa?" Mark sounded worried.

"It won't be the first time," Kate said matter-of-factly.

"Mama!" Karissa gave her mother a scolding look.

Mark looked between Kate and Karissa, neither of whom would return his gaze. "Was it Laura?"

Karissa closed her eyes and nibbled the cracker.

Kate stood and reached for the teakettle just before it whistled. She kept her back to Mark as she poured the steaming water over a tea bag. Slowly, she put two spoonfuls of sugar into the tea and stirred. *Laura? Who's Laura?* she wondered.

"Karissa, answer me." Mark was more insistent but still gentle. Kate couldn't help but wish Gerry knew how to be this gentle with his children.

"Mark, I don't . . . I mean, I don't . . . well . . ."

"You don't know, or don't *want* to know?"

"I guess I don't really know, but . . ."

"But. . . ?"

"I think so."

Mark swore under his breath.

"Mark!" Kate spun around, fearful that he was about to accuse Karissa of not being good enough for Michael. She needn't have worried.

"I told him more than once, a married man doesn't chase!" Mark was clearly agitated. "Kassy, I'm so sorry. I can't tell you how sorry I am." Mark covered his face with his hands and began to sob uncontrollably.

Kate and Karissa stared at each other in disbelief. Anger they understood; yelling they were used to. But this? A man weeping was totally new to both of them. Kate had never seen Gerry cry, and Karissa had seen Michael cry only once—when he had begged her to run away and marry him. When she'd finally agreed, his tears had dried as suddenly as his crying stopped. She had no idea she'd been manipulated.

"Mark, please, it's not your fault." Karissa moved to Mark's side.

"Oh, yes it is. I should have stopped him, somehow." Mark looked up into the tender expression of his son's young widow. "Oh, Kassy, I've lost Michael. Have I lost you too?"

Karissa put her arms around Mark's neck and pulled him close. As Kate had comforted her, Karissa now comforted Mark.

"No, Mark, and soon, the baby. Don't forget the baby."

"You're going to be a grandfather, Mark," Kate joined in.

"A 'papa,' " Karissa added. "That's what we call grandfathers in our family. Well, in my mother's family, anyway."

The anguish on Mark's face gave way to a look of joy. "Papa? Yeah, I like that." Then he became serious again. "Listen, Karissa, it's still not a good time to tell Phyllis. Not yet. I know we'll have to tell her eventually, but let's not do it until we absolutely have to, okay?"

"I'm all for that," Karissa said. "I don't look forward to her reaction. It will either be all negative or all positive. I don't know which I fear the most."

"For now, let's just keep this between us. Can we do that?"

"Well, not quite. Sandy and her parents know. And Mattie knows. But she's not about to say anything, and Sandy's family will keep quiet."

"Good. Now we have some practical issues to settle." Mark reached into his pocket and produced an envelope. "This will keep you going for a while. I need to let Phyllis have a little more time before I . . . well, we . . . change Michael's trust fund over to you, Karissa."

"Trust fund?"

"His grandfather—my father—left him quite a tidy sum. Phyllis has been the administrator of the fund for several years. I have been so busy building my business, she has managed all the household affairs and our personal finances for a long time. She's quite the good manager, too." Mark frowned. "I have to give her a little time before I begin to speak to her about . . . you know, financial things."

"Mark, I don't know what to say." Karissa appeared stunned by this new information.

"You didn't know?"

"I had no idea," Karissa said. "Michael didn't talk to me about money. He gave me a little household money for groceries and light bulbs, cleaning supplies, stuff like that."

"And for yourself, did he give you some money just to spend on yourself?"

"I guess if I needed anything he would have, but I really didn't need anything."

"What about the furniture, the redecorating?"

"Phyllis and Michael took care of everything. There was a decorator who picked out the wallpaper and the carpet. I didn't know what to pick. Phyllis has such good taste. I thought whatever she wanted would be fine with me."

"You like what she's done, then?"

"I never thought about it." Karissa shrugged.

Kate excused herself from the table and went into the living room. She looked around at Karissa's house. It was, at last, Karissa's—wasn't it?

"Mama?" Karissa followed Kate, and the two women had a moment alone together discussing the house.

"Kate"—Mark joined them in the living room— "listen to me. This house is supposed to be Karissa's home, not Phyllis's, and may God forgive me, it's not Michael's anymore. I have let things go too far for too long. As soon as I can, I will get this all settled. In the meantime, I will see to it that Karissa has everything she needs. Finances will not be a problem, believe me."

Turning to Karissa he said, "Can you be ready by two-thirty this afternoon? I need to take you to the bank and help you open a checking account."

"Mark, I don't—"

"She'll be ready," Kate interrupted. "Mind if I go along?"

"Not at all," Mark smiled at Kate. "I think that'd be a great idea." Then turning back to Karissa he asked, "Do you drive, Kassy?"

"Not really. I took driver's ed, but I—"

"Did you get your license?"

"Yes."

"Good, then don't hesitate to use the car. I left the keys on the kitchen counter a couple of days ago."

"I can't drive Michael's car." Karissa's face clouded with doubt.

"Of course you can." The anger in Mark's voice was rising once again. "It's your car too."

"No. I don't think so."

"When you got married, everything Michael owned became yours too."

"No, not really." She collapsed on the sofa and buried her face in her hands.

Mark and Kate exchanged glances, both at a loss to understand why Karissa felt as she did.

Mark didn't push her any further. Both he and Kate realized that so much had gone on behind the scenes between this young couple—things that they might never know. They needed to give Karissa time—time to find out who *she* was, and not who others wanted her to be.

"How long will you be able to stay, Kate?" Mark asked.

"I have to go home later this afternoon."

"Sandy's coming over to stay with me a few nights," Karissa said. "She's got her job, though, and her classes. She won't be here all the time."

"It's good that you'll have someone here with you at night," Mark nodded.

"Could we get that decorator back over here to finish the back bedroom?" Kate asked.

"Of course," Mark said. "I'll call him from the office."

"What shall I do with Michael's things?" Karissa asked the two of them.

"That's up to you, Karissa," Mark said. "Just don't put it off too long. It would be better if you had it all done by the time Phyllis—"

"I'll help her this morning," Kate jumped in. "We'll get a good start on it before this afternoon."

Kate turned and went to answer the phone ringing

in the kitchen. "It's Maria. She says Mrs. Andrews would like to speak to you."

"I'll call her back from the office. Tell Maria I'm leaving now." Mark gathered Karissa in his arms. "Listen, sweetheart, do whatever you want with Michael's things. Put them in boxes, and whatever you don't want, I'll take home. I'm sure Phyllis will know what to do with it all."

"I don't want anything, Mark."

"I understand." Mark lightly kissed the top of Karissa's head. "It's okay. Don't feel you have to keep anything you don't want to. Have you heard from your father?"

"No," Karissa said. "But then, I didn't expect to."

Kate quickly rushed to Karissa's side and put her arms around her daughter. "Thank you for all you've done, Mark. I don't know what we would have done without you."

Mark quietly left the two women alone.

———

*How could one young woman bear up under such pain and rejection?* Mark wondered as he headed to his office. *And how could Kate still be so lovely after having six children with such an uncaring, insensitive husband?* He immediately pushed that thought from his mind.

He had some serious issues to settle with Phyllis. It would be the most difficult thing he ever did, but Michael was gone now. How much more could he lose? Kassy, the baby? *Not on your life!* Mark thought. *She managed to separate me from my son, but she'll not come between me and Karissa—and the baby. I'm the baby's "papa"!*

# Five

Mark made his way home after seeing to it that Karissa had enough money in her new checking account to handle her needs until Michael's trust fund could be transferred into her name. He knew Phyllis wasn't going to be happy about what he had done. She wouldn't be happy about what had to be done still, but then she was very touchy when it came to matters of money. He had given in many years before and turned all responsibility for running the household and Michael's money over to her without interference. Trying to excuse himself from not standing up to her, he often shrugged it off by saying to himself and others that he only made the money—Phyllis's responsibility was to spend it. Unfortunately, she was better at spending than Mark liked, or even knew.

"I thought you were only working a short day." Phyllis's greeting was tinged with a whine.

"I'm home early, Phyl."

"It's almost five-thirty."

"I don't usually get home before seven."

"You never returned my call. I tried calling the office—you weren't there. Theresa didn't know where you went and didn't know when you'd be back."

"I went out."

"Obviously." Phyllis turned away, then looking back over her shoulder, she said, "I'll tell Maria we'll have an early dinner."

"Don't bother. I'm not hungry."

"Did you have a late lunch?" The question sounded a little too innocent.

Mark hadn't eaten any lunch. But after helping Karissa open her account, he had persuaded her and Kate to at least have some ice cream at the corner soda fountain.

"I'm not hungry." Mark wanted her to leave it at that. "I'll be in the den reading the paper."

"Fine," Phyllis pouted.

"Don't start, Phyllis."

"Start what?"

"I recognize that tone, and I'm not in the mood for it." Mark started toward the den.

"My son died less than a week ago and you have barely spoken a civil word to me since."

"You're wrong."

"Wrong? Michael's dead, isn't he? We haven't even discussed it, have we?" Her voice was pitched high and shrill. "You made all the arrangements without so much as consulting me. I might have wanted some things done differently. . . ."

"Stop it." Mark was not going to take this, not now. "First of all . . ." He dreaded where this conversation might lead. He took a deep breath and forced his voice to a calmer level. "First of all," he said quietly, "Michael wasn't *your* son, he was our son. Second, I couldn't discuss it with you. You were sleeping off all those pills."

"Well, what did you expect? How was I supposed to get through this tragedy? You don't know what it's like to be a real father, much less a mother!"

Mark closed his eyes against the emotional slap. He slowly took control of himself before facing his wife. "Third, we haven't spoken a civil word in this house for months. Why should the last few days be any different?" Mark was instantly sorry he had phrased that last remark as a question.

"Why? Because we've been dealt a terrible blow, that's why. We need to stick together, that's why. Because I need a husband by my side, that's why!" Phyllis began to sob uncontrollably. "I've lost my only child and you can't even find it in your heart to hold me."

Mark felt pity for her. Crossing the distance between them, he wrapped his arms around her and pulled her close. She stiffened and tried to resist. "Why fight me, then?" Mark asked as he tightened his hold on her. Finally, she relaxed against him and cried into his shoulder.

"We only have each other now," she said. "We better get used to the idea. It used to be good for us, Mark. Can't it be good again?"

"We don't have each other, Phyllis. You know that better than anyone. You threw away what we had long ago. Now that Michael's gone, we really have nothing." Mark was surprised at how calm he was. He had sealed off his heart from her incessant criticism and nagging long ago. She couldn't hurt him anymore, not without Michael to use.

"Don't say that, Mark darling. We can find each other again. We can comfort each other." Phyllis moved seductively against him, and Mark momentarily considered using her in much the same way as she had used him in the last few years.

Dropping his arms from around her, he stepped away, out of her reach. "Not on your life." Mark turned and crossed the large, expensively decorated living room toward the den. "Tell Maria I don't want any dinner."

Phyllis stamped her foot as she heard the den door close softly behind Mark. He was much more collected than she could remember recently, and she didn't like it when he was controlled. Something was not right. She couldn't put her finger on it, but Michael's death was not it. Mark and Michael had never been close—she had seen to that long ago. No, something else was not right; Mark was not himself. *Where were you today?* she asked silently. *What have you been up to?*

———

Gerry hadn't yet returned home from work when Mark dropped Kate off at the house. It felt good to be home, and she was glad for an hour or two to be with the kids before Gerry was due home. Helen had supper already in the oven, and in her own strict way she had the house in perfect order and the children fully under control.

"Thanks so much for coming," Kate said. "You are a blessing to us all." She knew she was taking a risk approaching Gerry's sister so warmly.

"Well, I couldn't stand by and see these children ignored just because . . ." Helen let her voice drop and then changed the subject. "Jodie got her finger smashed in a school desk. She blames the Mason boy, but I assured her that all she had to do was move her hand. She's a big girl. If no one is too soft on her, she'll be fine." She stared pointedly at Kate, then rattled on. "Sammy got a hundred on his spelling. He's very bright you know . . . all he needs is a little coaching. Ronnie is learning to ride his bicycle *without* the training wheels. Edie is upstairs in bed because she spilled her milk at lunch. Young ladies need to suffer some consequences for their clumsiness, you know. And Lisa went in the potty chair—finally!"

Helen hadn't changed a bit—every problem had an answer, every child had to be challenged to be better. Wasn't there anyone who believed, as Kate did, that children grow at their own rate and learn at their own speed?

How long had Helen drilled Sammy on his spelling? Had she even washed and kissed Jodie's hand? Did Ronnie ask for the training wheels to be taken off his bike? Didn't most four-year-olds spill milk at one time or another?

"How long did you make Lisa sit?"

"Pardon me?" Helen didn't like to be questioned about her child-training methods. She had never married or had children of her own, but she certainly knew how to raise them, and said so—far too often.

"How long did she sit on the potty chair?"

"It won't be so long next time, once she gets the hang of it. She's old enough to know what it's all about."

"It would help if she could say 'potty,' don't you think?"

"If she can say 'Mama,' she can learn to say 'potty.' Besides, if you'd put her on a schedule—"

"You mean set her on the potty every hour?"

"That would do for starters."

Kate shook her head and started upstairs to rescue her two youngest from their beds.

"You're too soft on them, Kathleen."

Kate stopped halfway up the stairs and turned to face her plain and rigid sister-in-law.

"Our family was—"

"I know how your family was, Helen." *For two decades I've lived with a man raised with only rules and no affection,* she thought to herself, tempted to scream at Helen and try to force her to see the truth about the rigid family she had come from. "Don't tell me how to raise my own children." Kate stood where she was, gripping the dark oak railing for control as she waited for Helen's retort.

"It just seems to me"—Helen always had to have

the last word—"that Karissa could've used a much firmer hand."

Kate closed her eyes and fought against the picture of her oldest daughter looking so hurt and alone. "Don't talk to me about Karissa. Her father used a firmer hand than was necessary and look—"

What was the use? The Hill family didn't believe in coddling or even in cuddling. A crying baby was never picked up until it was shushed first. The more control the better—that was the Hill family motto. Closeness and affection didn't prepare children for eventual separation.

"I wasn't speaking of her father, Kathleen. You're too soft on your children. Look at the trouble Karissa's in now. For goodness sake, face the truth. Karissa didn't know how to be a wife. If she had—"

"Stop it! You know nothing about Karissa or her marriage. You didn't even meet Michael." Kate felt all control leave as her body began to tremble with anger. "For your information, the lack of affection from her own father drove her into the arms of the first young man that gave her any attention at all."

"How dare you say such things to me about my brother—after all he's done for you! Giving you such a large family, this big house! Where's your appreciation for him?"

"I will not speak to you about this. My marriage and my family are my responsibility. I thanked you for coming, now I'll thank you to go—as soon as possible."

"Kathleen!" Gerald's voice rang from below. "I'll have you apologize to my sister this instant!"

"It's all right, Gerald." Helen's tone was thick with righteous martyrdom. "She's been through a bad time. She'll be back to her right self soon enough. She doesn't mean half of what she's saying."

Kate turned and hurried up the stairs. She could

hear the baby jumping in her crib and knew, after all,
babies *must not* enjoy themselves in their beds. *Nor
should adults for that matter.* Kate smiled. Helen,
poor Helen. If she could only see her self-controlled
brother when . . .

"Mama!" Lisa squealed. A dripping wet diaper
hung low between her knees. "Mama!" Kate picked
her up, wetness and all, and smothered her round
face with kisses. Carrying her over to Edie's bed, she
scooped the four-year-old into her embrace as well.
The three of them tumbled onto Edie's bed in one
large ball of hugs and kisses as the little girls
screamed and giggled.

*Gerald, will you abandon these two as you have
Karissa?* Suddenly, she pitied the distant and demanding man she had married.

As she cleaned up the children, Kate was glad to
have something to do before she faced Helen or Gerry
again. She could hear the voices of her older children
downstairs, probably gathered around the table doing homework or practicing their times tables or
spelling words. She knew she needed to be stricter
about their schoolwork, but she wanted them to have
more than just work and drilling in their young lives.
They would be grown and have long workdays soon
enough. Children needed to explore and discover, not
just drill and memorize. Neither Gerald nor Helen
agreed with her.

Kate insisted on keeping a couple of hens out
back. It was good for the children to have fresh eggs—
at least that's what she told Gerald. They also needed
to have contact with the chickens, but she kept that
thought to herself. Nothing was quite as delightful as
Ronnie's uproarious laugh when the chickens pecked
at the feed he so carefully spread around on the
ground. Kate mused over the memories of not only
the chickens but the guinea pigs and the rabbits.

The hutch was empty now. Gerald had drawn the line when he discovered a rabbit in Sammy's bed one night. Gerald didn't understand about rabbits and kids. He didn't understand kids, period. But Kate did, and she loved them, all six of them—soon to be seven with the new grandbaby on the way.

It would be a wonderful experience, having a new baby in the family that she didn't have to feed, change, and, above all, give birth to. It was Karissa's turn now. Kate would be a grandma soon. She was sure she'd love that just as much as she loved being a mother—maybe even more.

# Six

Karissa was glad to have Sandy with her in the small house, and the two friends became closer than ever. Sandy would be leaving to attend Claremont College second term, so Karissa would have to be ready to live alone by then. But for now, they settled into a routine.

"Excuse me. Mrs. Andrews?" The well-dressed man approached Karissa as she planted a few bulbs out in the backyard.

"Yes?"

"I'm Hal Walker, with the police department." He opened a wallet briefly to display a badge and then put it back in his coat pocket. "May I have a word with you?"

"Of course." Karissa stood, brushed her hands and knees off, and pushed a strand of hair back behind her ear. "Please sit down." She motioned toward the bright-colored patio settee.

"Thanks. Mrs. Andrews, I'm here about your husband's unfortunate accident. Let me extend my deepest sympathy."

"Thank you." Karissa sat opposite the detective. "What do you want to know?"

"I understand he went swimming after hours?"

"Yeah. They did that quite often. Once they even got caught, but no one made a big deal of it."

"They?"

"Michael and his friends."

"What friends?"

"I don't know for sure which ones went that night. Usually it was Jimmy Hernandez, Frankie Jordan, Rick Martin, and Hank Thomas. Bobby Johnson used to go too, but he joined the Marines last month."

"I see. Do you know for sure any of the guys that went with him that night?"

"Jimmy—he was with him here first." Karissa winced at the memory of that night.

"Jimmy Hernandez?"

"Yeah. Ricky came by, too. They met in the driveway, though—he didn't come in."

"Okay. Let me see. Jimmy and Michael were here at the house before they went . . . just exactly where did they go first, do you know?"

"No, I don't. Sometimes they went to play pool at Manny's. But I don't think they did that night."

"Why not?"

"Because Manny came by here looking for them. He asked me where they had gone. He seemed really mad that they had gone without him."

"Manny was mad?"

"Didn't want to be ditched—you know, left behind, I guess."

"Is that what he said?"

"No, I don't exactly remember what he said. When he came to the door I talked to him through the screen. I didn't really feel like seeing anybody. Michael and I had just had an argument. I was still upset."

"I see . . ." Walker paused to scribble a few words on his note pad. "Then what happened?"

"Manny opened the screen and stepped inside. He got real mad and called Michael a . . . well, a bad name. I told him they left earlier, and I didn't know where they were. He asked if I was all right, I said I was, and he left." Karissa remembered clearly the expression on Manny's face. He was almost as mad as Michael. She couldn't understand why Manny was so angry over simply being left behind. He knew where they all hung out; she was sure he'd find them without much trouble.

"What's this all about, anyway?" Karissa asked.

"It's pretty routine, really. We run an investigation whenever there is . . . well, whenever . . ."

"It's okay, Mr. Walker. Michael died while doing something he wasn't supposed to. It was pretty much the same way he lived."

"I guessed as much. He must have had a good job, though." Walker nodded at the house. "You renting?"

"No, Michael's parents gave us a large down payment for the house so we could afford to buy it."

"Nice." Walker made a few more notes.

"Yeah, well"—Karissa looked around the yard—"it'll be a lot of work. But I have a little brother; I'm hoping I can get him to help me mow the lawn."

"You're planning to stay here alone, then?"

"Not really. I have a friend staying with me—for now anyway. I'll have to make some decisions later. Right now though . . ."

"Give yourself time, Mrs. Andrews," Walker said gently. He stood and looked steadily at Karissa. "I may have more questions later, Mrs. Andrews. Would you be willing to answer them?"

Why did she have the feeling Mr. Walker didn't completely believe her? "I don't really know anything more, but I'll try," she offered.

Walker turned and walked toward the edge of the yard, then turned back to ask, "Know where I can find Manny?"

"Home, I guess. I don't know. I haven't seen him since that night."

"What's Manny's last name?"

"Rodriguez. Manuel Rodriguez. His dad owns the

Standard station over on High Street. He may be working there. He does sometimes."

Mr. Walker thanked Karissa and got into his car.

Lost in her own thoughts, she stood looking after the detective as he pulled out of her driveway and went down the road. Karissa didn't hear Mattie Sloan approaching the chain link fence separating their yards.

"Kassy?"

"Oh, Mattie, hello!"

"How're you doing, my dear?"

"Pretty well, thanks. I'm getting stronger every day. It's been two weeks already."

"How's that nasty eye?"

"Much better. I guess I haven't thanked you for coming over that night. I can't tell you—"

"Don't even try, Karissa. That's what neighbors are for."

"Can I make you some iced tea?" Karissa needed company right then. She couldn't say why, but she had felt suddenly alone after the detective left.

"My, that does sound good, now, doesn't it? I'll be right back."

Karissa went into her small kitchen and got out the tall, frosty yellow glasses and the big pitcher from the ice box. She kept the glasses cold because Mark had suggested chilled glasses didn't melt the ice as fast. She didn't have a glass chiller like they did in their bar, but she could at least have them cold.

A minute later Mattie came in the back door carrying a few fresh lemons off the tree in her backyard. "Thought these might come in handy," she said as she settled into a chair opposite Karissa.

"I've wanted to thank you before this," Karissa said, "but I've just been—"

"Honey, my goodness. You don't have to apologize to me. You've been busy. I know that. Your mama was here, and your father-in-law. I met them—they seem like such nice folks."

"Then that decorator," Karissa offered. "It took him almost a week to finish that one little bedroom."

"How'd it turn out?"

"Sandy's staying in it. It sure helps to have someone else here at night."

"I saw her this morning. What a lovely girl."

"You want to see the room?"

"I'd like to see what you've done to the whole place."

"Well, I didn't really do it," Karissa said. "Michael's mother picked out all the wallpaper and paint and stuff. Her house is beautiful. She's much better at this than I am."

Mattie followed Karissa into the living room for a tour of the house.

"The furniture is all handed down from Michael's parents. After they helped us buy the house, Mrs. Andrews bought new furniture and gave us their old things. Far better than anything I'd ever seen before. I never dreamed of having such a nice place to live."

"It *is* lovely, dear. Not many young people get to set up housekeeping in such style. Now how about you? I see you're not limping anymore. That ankle better?"

"Much. I keep this wrap on it and take it off at night. I try to keep it up part of the day. That's when I watch *The $64,000 Dollar Question*."

"I do the same thing!" Mattie laughed. "It's my favorite show."

"I finally got the washer hooked up in the garage. It was finished just a day or two before—"

"You get one of those new automatics?" Mattie asked.

"Yeah, my mother says I'm spoiled."

"It's the thing now. I'll get one someday. Ben is determined."

Karissa was grateful for Mattie's company. The elderly woman's cheerful smile and friendly conversation lifted her spirits. After showing her neighbor around the house, the two women returned to the kitchen to finish their iced tea.

"How long have you been married, Mattie?"

"Well, let's see. I guess we've been married almost forty-five years now. When we hit fifty, we're going on another honeymoon."

"Really? A second honeymoon . . . that's wonderful."

"Oh no, not a second, a fiftieth—we call every trip we ever take a honeymoon." Mattie laughed. "Ben is such a romantic old fool."

"And children? How many children do you have?"

"We had four, but we lost all of them. Two died when they were babies. Then my daughter Patricia went to be with the Lord when she was only five—diphtheria. And Paul fought in World War II. He died somewhere in Italy." Mattie grew wistful.

"I'm sorry, Mattie." Karissa had no idea her neighbors had experienced such pain.

"Ben and I have always had each other." Mattie smiled at Karissa. "And, we have the Lord. He's really what has kept us going. In the middle of our greatest sorrow, He has always managed to open a door of hope."

Karissa straightened suddenly and felt the blood drain from her face.

"Honey, have I said something . . ."

"That's what the young minister said at Michael's funeral. I almost forgot. Please wait right here. I want to show you something."

Karissa ran into the bedroom and retrieved the white card from underneath her pillow. She didn't know why, but having that card nearby to touch during the night brought her a measure of comfort.

"See? He gave me this."

"Who did, dear?"

"His name is Jim Henry. Mark knows him well. He said a few words at the cemetery. See, his church is listed on the other side. River Place Community."

Mattie smiled. "Pastor Jim."

"You know him?"

"He's my pastor. River Place is my church."

"Your church? I never knew there was a church at that address. Isn't that a school?"

"It's a school during the week, but on Sunday, we make it the house of the Lord." She smiled. "It's quite exciting. In fact, we're going to have our own building soon. We've just bought property out on the edge of town. We'll be breaking ground before long. Maybe even as early as next spring if all goes well and the money comes in."

"I sleep with this under my pillow." Karissa fingered the card.

"Oh?" Mattie reached for the hand of the younger woman. "Why is that, dear?"

"It's the strangest thing, Mattie. Sometimes I wake up and I think Michael is still coming home later or something. I can't quite get used to the idea that he's . . . dead." Karissa's eyes filled with tears.

"It takes a while for the reality to set in, honey. You have to give it time."

"I can't get used to it, Mattie. But those times I think he'll be coming in any minute, drunk or mad at me for something, I get afraid all over again. It takes me a few minutes to remember he's not . . . ever . . ." Karissa laid her head on her arms.

"Was he often angry at you, Karissa?"

"All the time." Karissa raised her head and reached for a paper napkin to wipe her nose. "I tried to make him happy, Mattie, but I just couldn't do it. I just couldn't."

"No one can make anyone happy, dear. Happiness comes from inside. It's each person's responsibility to make themselves happy."

"But I disappointed him. . . . I must have disappointed him. He was always so unhappy. Before we married—we ran away the night of January Jubilee prom night—he wanted . . . well, he said being married would make him so happy. But it didn't."

"And your parents?"

"We didn't tell anyone until after I graduated."

"You kept your marriage a secret?"

"Michael wanted to keep it secret even longer. He wanted me to wait until September. But I couldn't. I told my mother."

"And then what happened?"

"She just cried and held me close. She went to Michael's father's office one day and told him. He hit the roof!" Karissa smiled. "He wasn't mad at me, but he was really mad at Michael.

"Later that same day Michael stormed into my parents' house and stared down my father while I got my things. We went to a motel that night and the next day we moved into an apartment." Karissa twisted the paper napkin in her hands. "That first night was the first night he left me alone and went out and got drunk."

"Oh, my dear." Mattie's voice broke as she patted Karissa's hand.

"I didn't know what to do. He was so mad at me for telling my mother. He said he wanted to handle it in his own way, in his own time. He said it was bad enough trying to deal with his own mother, but now to have an interfering mother-in-law too, well, that was the last straw. That night was awful. He hit me real hard and I locked myself in the bathroom until he calmed down."

Karissa quickly filled Mattie in on the rest of the story. How Phyllis had eventually calmed down—after becoming convinced the marriage couldn't be annulled—then had set about making all the plans for a proper wedding. Karissa remembered her own mother's sudden flash of temper when Phyllis suggested it. As Karissa recalled the entire situation and shared it with Mattie, she realized she admired her mother's determination to keep Phyllis from making a "complete fool of us all."

"Why was your mother upset about having a wedding?"

"She said the marriage had already happened, that to go through it again was ridiculous. She agreed that a reception was appropriate, but not a wedding."

"I think I agree," Mattie said.

"I didn't care, I only wanted peace."

Karissa paused and took a long drink of her iced tea. "I guess I shouldn't have told Mama. But she knew something was wrong. She thought I was having . . . well, doing wrong things with Michael. I had to tell her. I didn't do anything until we were married. That made Michael mad, too."

"And the night he died he . . . he was angry that night too, wasn't he?"

"The worst ever. He was mad at me because of the . . . because I . . ." Karissa paused, took a deep breath, and then continued. "Mattie, I'm going to have a baby."

"Karissa! How wonderful!" Mattie seemed genuinely happy at this news.

"Michael was furious when I first told him about the baby. After that he never really wanted to talk about it. That night I guess I pushed him too far. He blamed me for it—but Mattie, I didn't mean to get pregnant. I really didn't." Karissa's eyes filled with tears again.

"Listen, sweetheart. God loves that little baby inside you. You know that, don't you? God's not mad about that."

"My father doesn't know yet. Neither does Michael's mother." Karissa didn't acknowledge Mattie's words of God's love for the unborn child. She sighed. "I don't know why they can't just all leave me alone now. I'm happy about the baby. Michael didn't want it . . . I even thought he might be trying to beat it out of me that night. He didn't want it, but I do. I really do." Karissa looked at Mattie and smiled through her tears.

"When are you going to tell Mrs. Andrews?"

"I don't know. I haven't even seen her except at the funeral. She hasn't called but once or twice looking for Mark."

"Well, dear, don't you worry. I'm sure things will work out somehow with your mother-in-law. Time has a way of healing these things." She stood and gave Karissa a warm hug. "I'd better be going now . . . but you call me if you need anything. Anything at all."

# Seven

"Where are Michael's things?" Phyllis's voice was shrill and put Mark's teeth on edge. "I want his things brought home!"

"I don't have them, Phyl, I've told you." Mark and Phyllis had had this same argument several times in the past few days.

"I want my son's things brought home. Do you hear me?" Phyllis was getting angrier than Mark had seen her since Michael's death.

"I don't have the right to go into Karissa's garage and get them." Mark regretted saying the words the very moment he spoke them.

"The garage?" Phyllis shrieked.

"Calm down, Phyllis. Karissa packed his things neatly, I assure you."

"Then you've seen them?"

"Get hold of yourself, woman!"

"I will not get hold of myself. I want my son's personal belongings. Is that too much to ask? My only son is dead. All I want is his things. She doesn't care about them any more than she cared about Michael. I want to put them back in his room. She never loved him—why should she care about his things?" Phyllis walked stiffly behind the wet bar in the living room and refilled her glass.

"Let it alone, Phyllis. You've had quite enough to drink already."

"I want Michael's things, do you hear me? I will go

over there myself and get them. She won't wrap me around her little finger as she obviously does you! Not me! I want his things and I intend to have them. Is that clear?"

"Let me do it," Mark sighed and resigned himself to asking Karissa rather than having Phyllis hurt her—or worse, find out about the baby. "I'll do it tomorrow the first thing after lunch, okay?"

"I warn you, Mark Andrews. If you don't get his things tomorrow, I'll be over there the first thing day after. Do you understand me?"

"I understand you." Mark took a deep breath and let it out again slowly. Why couldn't Phyllis understand him for a change? He felt as much pain as she did. It was only the thought of Karissa and the baby that kept him going at all. But poor Phyllis, she didn't even have that. She would have to know soon, of course—he knew that—but he would hide it from her as long as possible. She would know only after he could warn Karissa.

How do you tell someone to keep a baby away from its own grandmother? Karissa wouldn't think of keeping Kate away from the baby. Why should she? Kate was a wonderful mother and would be a devoted grandmother. Mark shoved thoughts of Kate from his mind. It wasn't right, the thoughts he had of her. He pushed those same thoughts from his mind countless times each day.

So far, he had managed to keep from running into her at Karissa's. He hadn't really tried to avoid her; in fact, once or twice he had stopped by hoping to find her there. Karissa always made some excuse, saying her mother had been there a day or two before, or that she wasn't expecting her until tomorrow. Mark didn't push for information about Kate for fear Karissa might suspect just how much he hoped to see her.

———

"It's been almost two weeks, Gerry," Kate cried late that same night. "She's my oldest daughter, she's just lost her husband, and I can't even get three miles across town to see how she's doing."

"She's doing fine." Gerald's tone was matter-of-fact and calm.

"And how do you know?" Kate knew Gerald didn't like being questioned. In fact, questioning his judgment, or his opinion, or his word had, more than once, brought a stinging slap across Kate's face. But tonight she didn't care. Tonight all she thought of was Karissa.

"I said, I know!"

Gerald's eyes snapped with anger and Kate knew that if she pushed just a little more she might feel the back of his hand.

"You obviously didn't hear me, did you, Kathleen?"

"Yes, Gerald, I did. But you obviously didn't hear *me*." Kate trembled, knowing she was going too far. "I think it's time you heard me for a change."

Gerald raised his hand and Kate raised her voice. "In fact, it's past time, Gerry! I'm telling you this, and I'm only telling you once."

Gerald stopped with his hand in midair, poised to bring the back of it across Kate's mouth.

"You hit me—you *ever* hit me again, and I swear it will be the last time. Do you hear me, Gerald?" Kate's voice had dropped suddenly to a calm and even tone.

"Don't you talk to me like—"

"I'm not going to take it anymore, Gerald Hill. You can quote Bible verses at me all you want. You can yell and scream that I should be submissive and subject to you. But you know something, Gerry? I can read too. And there's a Bible verse that comes right after those about wives submitting themselves to their own husbands. Do I have to read it to you? Or do you trust me to remember it correctly?" Kate grabbed Gerry's big black leather Bible off the dresser. Gerald stood shocked and motionless.

"It says it right here—I underlined it so you wouldn't have to look too hard for it." Kate pointed to Ephesians 5:25. "Right here, Gerry. God's Word says a husband is to love his wife as Christ loved the church and gave himself up for her. It says you are to love me as Jesus loves all of us. Do you love me like that, Gerry?"

Gerald grabbed for the Bible and Kate dodged out of his reach. "Oh, my husband, there is even more. The Bible says husbands ought to love their wives as they love their own bodies. Is that how you treat your own body? Do you slap yourself across the face whenever you have a confusing thought or question yourself about something?" Kate found the anger pouring freely from her aching heart and empty soul. "It says a husband is to nourish and cherish, Gerry. Is that what you do when you slap me? Are you nourishing me? Are you cherishing me?"

"Kathleen, stop it. How dare you use the Word of God to—"

"To sound like you? How come when I quote it I'm *using* it, and when *you* quote it you're being holy and righteous?"

"I do nothing of the sort," Gerry retorted, his voice beginning to thicken with anger. "I'm the head of this house, Kathleen. I have to maintain my headship here."

"The head of the house never has to maintain his position any more than Jesus has to maintain His position as the Son of God." Kathleen knew the Bible well and read it daily. She never saw Gerald open his Bible except at church or when he was trying to keep her or one of the children in line—usually before he whipped one of the children or slapped her.

"Don't try to teach me the Bible, woman!" Gerald's eyes once again snapped with anger.

"Oh yes. I forgot. A woman can only *ask* her husband at home. Okay, then, husband, I'm asking . . . why should I stay with a husband who believes the Bible only applies to those weaker than himself? Why should I listen to the words and the direction of a man who disregards the directions of the Word of God for himself?"

"Stop it, Kathleen, I'm warning you!"

Kate stepped away from him. "Disregards the directions of God's Word for himself but insists that the rest of us follow it to the letter?"

Gerald lunged at his wife, but she quickly stepped out of the way, and he stumbled and fell against the lamp table near the window. As he came quickly to his feet, Kate could see he was angrier than she had ever seen him. He flew at her and she bolted from the room.

For the twenty-one years she had been married to Gerald, she had managed to keep all their disagreements confined to their bedroom. Now she entered the bedroom of her two sons, fourteen-year-old Sammy and eight-year-old Ronnie. The two boys sat up in bed, startled by their mother's sudden entrance. Gerald burst into the room and grabbed for his wife's arm.

"No!" Kate screamed. "I won't take it anymore. If you're going to hit me, do it here, in front of your sons! Let them know how a Christian man treats his wife!" Kate sobbed hysterically. Sammy immediately stood at her side to protect her.

"Stand aside, son," Gerald said calmly.

"No, Dad, I won't. You think we don't hear you in your room? We know you hit her. We know you hit

Kassy and Jodie, too. You whip all of us." Sammy stood almost as tall as his mother but was still a full six inches shorter than his father.

"That's enough, Samuel, this is between your mother and me."

"Not anymore, Dad. Now it's between us all." Sammy motioned toward the doorway, where Jodie stood holding Edie by the hand and Lisa in her arms.

"Mama!" Lisa wailed at her mother, stretching her hands toward Kate. "Mama!"

"Stop that infernal screeching!" Gerald spun toward his daughters. Jodie ducked past him, pulling Edie along. The moment Lisa could reach her mother, she flung herself into Kate's arms. Gerry turned toward his family as he backed toward the door. "You've shamed me in front of my children, Kate. I won't forget this. I don't think I can forgive you for this."

"Mama!" Lisa pulled on Kate's face, trying to force her mother to look at her.

"Shh. Shh, baby," Kate soothed without taking her eyes from Gerald's. "If anyone's shamed you, Gerry, I think you ought to look in the mirror."

She had waited years before taking this stand. She had never planned to take it—and she certainly didn't plan on ever having to take it again. "I've been the submissive wife for over twenty years, Gerry. Now it's your turn. For the next twenty you can be the loving, sacrificing husband."

Gerry turned suddenly and slammed the door behind him as he left the room. Kate and the children stood silently together and listened to Gerald stomp out the back door, start the car, and hastily pull out of the driveway.

Kate slumped to the floor and dissolved into tears. Her stunned children gathered around her. Lisa and Edie snuggled close to their mother, and the older children hugged and patted her, trying to comfort her. Regaining control of herself, Kate tried to calm and reassure her children.

After a few minutes, she put them all back to bed and tried not to think about what Gerry would do or say when he returned. She made her way quietly downstairs and heated water for tea. She jumped when she heard a noise behind her. "Oh, Margie, it's you. You startled me!"

"Your bedroom windows are open, Kate."

"You heard?"

"The whole neighborhood heard." Margie pulled out a chair opposite Kate. "You all right?"

"I'm all right. At least for now. I'm not sure what I just did, but I know I'm twenty years too late."

"It's never too late. Pastor Jim said—"

"Pastor Jim?"

"You know, the new pastor over at that little church in the school. The one who spoke at the funeral. Well, he said it's never too late."

"I hope he's right, Margie. I hope he's right."

"Where'd Gerry go?"

"I don't have the slightest idea." Kate sighed and, leaning forward on her arms, let her tears flow freely. Margie's comforting hand on her shoulder somehow assured her she wasn't alone.

Half an hour later Margie left, and Kate went systematically from door to door, turning the key in each lock. She left the keys in the locks, turned halfway so that no one could get a key in the other side. Climbing the stairs to her room, she felt exhausted and weary beyond her forty years.

Shutting her bedroom door behind her, she locked that door as well. She was going to get a good night's sleep tonight. She didn't want to be disturbed.

Jodie would take care of the little ones if necessary. And Gerald—well, Gerald would just have to take care of himself—wherever he was.

# Eight

Summerwind, a sleepy little town snuggled in the rich fertile valley just below the foothills of the San Gabriel Mountains, was at one time considered an oasis for the wealthy who came to escape the harsh winters of the northern central states.

Real estate had been cheap when this gentle land was undeveloped. Water was all it took to get anything to grow there. The mild winters and hot summers proved to be ideal for growing the best and biggest oranges. Orange plantations soon sprawled for miles in all directions. The navels were harvested every December, and the Valencias were picked every summer. The groves provided steady industry and gave the valley floor a lush green appearance in contrast to the barren mountaintops above.

Like so many others, Gerald Hill had come to Summerwind to escape the city and raise his family in a small-town atmosphere. Many of the older orange groves had already been pulled out and the land sold to a new generation more interested in housing developments than orange growing and packing. The new construction industry had given him plenty of work. He was an electrician by trade, and one of the best.

Most contractors sought him out. He was not only meticulous in his work but insisted that no corners be cut when it came to passing inspections and meeting codes. It was good steady work and he worked hard. Maybe even harder than most. That's why he was in demand. People could count on him—they knew it and he knew it.

But tonight, driving around the familiar town long after most people were in bed sleeping, Summerwind offered him no comfort. Driving by the job sites where he was often complimented on the quality of his work gave him no satisfaction. Kate hated him. He was sure of it. And because she did, nothing else mattered.

He glanced at the big black Bible lying on the seat beside him. He had tried so hard to be a good provider. He had taken his family to church each Sunday. Nothing swelled his chest with pride more than seeing Kate and their six nearly filling the pew each Lord's day. Seeing the Bible there on the seat, he almost wished he hadn't picked it up on his way out.

He didn't want to look at the places she had underlined, but pulling over under a nearby streetlamp, he began leafing through the nearly untouched pages. How long had he owned it? Twenty-one years? It had been Kate's first Christmas present to him after they were married. Kate was not as careful with her holy book. Hers was worn and some pages had been torn by little hands; she had often read from it while holding the babies. He caressed the book in his hands and shut his eyes against the pain from Kate's words, still stinging deep within.

She had time to spend in its pages each day. Gerald had his work, his family to support. He had learned years ago to rely on the words of each Sunday's sermon to sustain him throughout the week. *That's what ministers are for—in fact, that's what they're paid for.* Gerald had been careful that his ten percent—to the penny—went into the offering plate each week. He saw to that and, indeed, let others see it as well.

But now, with Kate's latest outburst, he had lost face in front of the children. How could he ever hold his head up again? He wasn't respected at home, and he wouldn't be in the church, either. It was a good thing he had his job. . . .

Gerald's eyes ran over the words Kate had underlined. When had she done that? It could have been five years or five days ago. She might have done it before she gave the Bible to him for Christmas. He had no way of telling. He hadn't ever really opened it except to follow along with the minister's text each Sunday.

In the dim light of the streetlamp, he read the words over and over again, trying to see what Kate had seen. He closed his eyes for a moment and without thinking, simply said, "Dear God, help me see this, help me understand what in the world the woman is talking about." His simple prayer gave way to deep sobs. Gerald couldn't remember crying since the day his own father scolded him for crying when his grandma died.

"We'll see her in heaven, son. No use cryin' and feelin' sorry for yourself now. Straighten yourself up, here, and be a little man. Big boys don't cry. Your mama needs us to be strong."

That was the last time Gerald had cried—until tonight. Sitting alone in his car, somewhere on a side street in Summerwind after midnight, Gerald broke. His daddy didn't say anything to him this time. It probably wouldn't have mattered to him anyway. The tears were too many, the pain too deep. Tonight, all alone in the darkness, Gerald wept openly and without reservation. Crushed by the prospect of losing Kate, Karissa, the kids—his whole world—he cried himself to sleep.

"Good morning, Sandy." Gerald's unkempt appearance caught the young woman off guard. His khaki work clothes were rumpled, his brown hair hung uncharacteristically over his forehead, and he obviously hadn't washed or shaved.

"Hello." Sandy glanced carefully over her shoulder toward Karissa's bedroom door.

"Karissa here?" Gerald mumbled.

"She's still asleep, Mr. Hill." Sandy didn't want to go off to work leaving Karissa alone with her father. Having lived next door to the Hills for most of her life, Sandy knew him to be a firm man—even given to temper. Seeing her father this early in the morning was not what Karissa needed—or could handle. Sandy knew that as soon as Karissa's feet hit the floor, she would need at least half an hour before morning sickness would allow her to leave the bathroom.

"Can I just wait inside, then?" Mr. Hill looked sheepish.

"Gee, I don't know." Sandy stood firmly in the doorway.

"What's the trouble here?" Sandy heard Mark's voice before she saw him coming up the walk behind Gerald Hill.

"I want to see my daughter." Gerald turned on the step to face Mark.

"I see," Mark said, eyeing Gerald suspiciously. "Well, Sandy, is Karissa even up yet?"

"Not yet."

"Well then, Hill, I guess you'll just have to come back another time."

"And just when did you assume responsibility for my daughter, Andrews?" Gerald's voice contained more hurt than anger.

"When she married my son, Hill. And even more

so when he died." Mark was struggling to keep his anger under control.

"I see."

"Good. Then you won't mind if we tell Karissa you came by, and *if* she is willing to see you, where can you be reached? Can I call you, let's say sometime later this afternoon, or even tomorrow?"

"We don't have a phone."

"So I've heard."

"What do you mean by that?"

"You don't have a phone, that's all." Mark's answer was clipped and direct.

"Had no use for one."

"I see, and your family? Do you suppose they might have had a use for one?" Mark seemed intent on goading the pitiful man into an argument. Then with visible effort, Mark forced himself to speak more civilly.

"Listen, Mr. Hill. Karissa's been through too much already. She doesn't need to see you like this. Go on home. I'll tell her you were by. Let's see how she reacts to that before we . . ."

Gerald turned and walked back to his car, leaving Mark's comment hanging in midair above the sidewalk.

Mark and Sandy watched him go, his shoulders slumped in defeat under his wrinkled blue work shirt.

"How sad," Mark mumbled. "He's lost his daughter. Doesn't he know it's too late?"

"It's never too late," Sandy said. "Remember what Pastor Jim said a few weeks ago?"

"Yeah, I do." Mark had begun attending the small church the very first Sunday after Michael's death. "I sure do. Let's hold on to that, shall we, Sandy? It's never too late."

————

Mark made himself at home in Karissa's kitchen, washing up Sandy's cereal bowl and putting on the teakettle for Karissa's morning tea. He had become quite familiar with the kitchen and enjoyed having the freedom to do so. In his own home, Maria was expected to wait on him—even if he didn't want her to. There was never any time to be alone, and in spite of the spaciousness of his house, there was no private place to think or even to pray, as he had been wanting to do lately. He hadn't, only because he thought he might be discovered. Mark didn't want to give Phyllis anything to mock or tease him about.

Mark took over being with Karissa when Sandy had to go to work. He usually stopped by the office first and gave his men their instructions for the day, and then disappeared for a few hours each morning to be with Karissa so she wouldn't be alone while she was so sick. Mark was afraid she'd fall or faint and need attention.

"Hello there!" Mattie's cheerful voice announced her usual morning visit. She would be glad to stay with Karissa, and Mark would be glad to let her—in time. But for now, she just came by to check on things, in case a woman's touch was needed.

"Mattie, come on in."

"Who was that at the door earlier?" Mattie asked.

"Karissa's father." Mark slowly sipped his cup of coffee.

"Oh, really? He looked pretty rough. Had he been out all night?"

"Looked that way, didn't it?" The phone rang and Mark reached for it before it could ring twice and wake Karissa. "Hello?"

"Hello. This is Kate Hill. I'm calling Karissa. I'm sorry, have I dialed the wrong number?"

"No, Kate, this is Mark."

"Mark. Good morning. I'm at the Smiths'—Sandy's parents. Is Kassy there?"

"She's still sleeping, I'm afraid. Do you want me to wake her?"

"I'm not sure that would be a good idea. She probably won't feel too well the first thing when she wakes up."

"That's why I'm here," Mark said. "I go on duty when Sandy goes to work."

"I see." Kate laughed, and Mark liked the way it sounded. "And are you filling in as a mother figure?" Kate went on.

"Sort of, but I have help. Mattie Sloan is here with me. She's the neighbor." Mark heard Kate take a deep breath on the phone. "Kate? You still there?"

"I'm here, but I should be there, Mark. I should be able to be with my daughter."

"You want me to come and get you?"

"No, but thanks. Listen, tell Karissa I'll be calling her later—about ten-thirty. How's that? Will she be up by then?"

"Not only up, I think she'll even have her feet beneath her by then."

"Well, then . . ."

"Kate?"

"Yes?"

"Gerald was by a few minutes ago."

"Oh?"

"Everything okay?"

"Why do you ask, Mark?"

"He looked pretty rough. Like he'd been up all night."

"He might have been."

"You don't know?"

"Not for sure. Just tell Karissa I'll be calling later. And, Mark, give her a—"

"A couple of crackers and a cup of tea. I know, I have my orders." Mark laughed and knew he mustn't enjoy talking to Kate so much. If Gerald couldn't see what he had in Kate, the man was blind. If he didn't appreciate her, he was crazy. Mark forced himself to think about something else.

# Nine

With each passing week, as her life took on some form and secure structure, Karissa felt stronger. She almost was convinced to visit River Place Community Church with Sandy and her parents. Mark was attending regularly now too, and he was also encouraging her to try it out. She knew Mattie and Ben would be more than willing to have her ride with them. Soon, maybe. Just as soon as she could be sure she wouldn't throw up in the service.

She talked with her mother often. She loved the friendly banter and chitchat tone of her mother's voice. She noticed her mother sounded different, at peace, and she wondered what had happened. She had even promised Karissa she would be over soon. The children had been taking turns coming down with the stomach flu, and Kate didn't want to expose Karissa to anything she could catch that might upset her stomach any more than it already was.

"Yoo-hoo!" It was Mattie's now-familiar greeting that woke Karissa one afternoon as she dozed in front of the TV.

"In the living room, Mattie."

"Don't get up, Karissa dear. I'm only going out for a few minutes and wanted you to know that I'd be gone."

"Don't worry about me so much. I'll be fine."

"Need anything, dear? I'm going to the A&P."

Karissa gave her dear elderly friend a small list

and the money for the few items. The two women walked out the back door and Mattie surveyed the yard.

"You could use some help here, couldn't you?"

"I was hoping my little brother could come and help me, but he's been quite sick with the flu. I guess it'll just have to wait."

"Nonsense. I have a splendid idea. I have a nephew who is a gardener. Every week or so he sees to it that our yard is taken care of. Let me speak to him. I'm sure he would be glad to give you a hand."

"I couldn't do that, Mattie. He's your nephew. I can understand why he would want to take care of yours. But you can't go around volunteering him for your neighbors. Thank you anyway."

"Pooh. Let me at least talk to him. Okay? Let him say no if he can't do it." Mattie waved at Karissa on her way down the driveway. "I'll speak to him."

"Mattie!"

"See you after a while, my dear." Mattie hurried to her car and drove away, leaving Karissa standing on her back step, smiling.

A few days later, as she worked in the flower bed, Karissa realized she was feeling stronger than she had since before she and Michael got married. She enjoyed her little house and had discovered she liked puttering around in the backyard, even though she was afraid to tackle the lawn mowing. The late afternoon and early evening was her favorite time. The backyard was shaded by the house and hosing down the small patio seemed to cool the entire area. While the afternoons were still quite warm, the October evenings were perfect.

Her pleasant phone conversations with Kate continued, but Edie had come down with German measles. Kate thought it best not to come visit until the rash completely cleared up. By then they would know if Lisa would also get them. Karissa was disappointed at first, but then contented herself with the phone calls every other day or so.

"Excuse me?"

The man's sudden interruption startled Karissa and she looked up from where she was kneeling next to the flower bed. "I'm sorry. I didn't hear anyone coming."

"I thought so. You were lost in your own thoughts." The tall, light-haired man smiled at Karissa. "Am I interrupting?"

"No, of course not." Karissa felt suddenly shy that she could be discovered so deep in thought and not at all paying attention to her surroundings. It was like that when she dug around the geraniums or the two small rosebushes she was trying to coax along out by the back fence.

"I guess I should introduce myself. I'm Holden Kelley."

Karissa didn't remember hearing his name before.

"My aunt Mattie sent me over. She said a little help was needed over here with the yard."

"Oh, Mattie!" Karissa hadn't remembered Mattie bringing up the subject since that one afternoon. Karissa had completely dismissed the idea.

"I can see she was right."

"Well, I'm kind of new at this. I don't think I can mow, but I can do everything else myself. I'm just trying to make it all look—well, neat." Karissa nodded toward the yard. "It was kind of overgrown when we moved in, and I've been trying to make some sense of it all. There's even a couple of old rosebushes at the back."

"Mind if I take a look?"

"I'm sorry," Karissa said, standing up and brushing off her sundress. "Come on in. Mattie says you're a gardener."

"That's right"—Holden smiled—"a gardener." Karissa caught sight of his even white teeth and the dimple in his cheek that appeared when he smiled. His tanned forehead spoke loudly of summer days spent outdoors.

"And where do you garden?"

"Well, here and there. I . . ." Holden paused. "Look at this, will you?" He squatted to have a closer look at Karissa's rosebushes. "You'll have a bud here before long. And it's October. These poor plants have been starving for attention. They're so grateful, they might even produce all winter for you—if you let them."

"Let them?" Karissa knew nothing about the intricacies of raising roses.

"They really should be cut back and deep fed before the cooler weather sets in. You could let them go awhile longer, if you want to. But soon, you should be looking at nothing but stubs. If, that is, you want beautiful roses in the spring."

"Cut them back?" Karissa could barely stand the thought.

"It's called pruning."

"Oh, yeah. I guess it's important, huh? Sort of a shame, though. They were so forlorn and scraggly. I hate to tease them with new growth then hack them back. Can they take the shock?"

"Oh, I think so." Holden's eyes twinkled as he smiled at Karissa. He didn't look away for several seconds, and Karissa felt at a loss for words.

"Well, how about it?" Holden broke the silence. "Is your mother home? I'd like to arrange a time I can come and do the mowing. Could use some fertilizer this time of year, too."

"My mother?" Karissa stared at Holden, thinking he was quite possibly the most handsome man she had ever seen. "What's my mother got to do with this?"

"I just thought I should speak to her. If it's too soon . . . I mean Mattie told me about . . . well, you know, being a new widow and all."

"No, my mother's not here. I can take care of this. I don't think we need to bother her. Believe me, this yard is not on her list of priorities."

"How well I know. Routine things can be a real help, though, during the rough days. I'm glad, at least, that you've taken some interest in the yard."

"Mr. Kelley, I think you misunderstand."

"I'm sorry?"

"My mother is not a widow. At least I don't think she is."

"But I thought—well, no matter what I thought. I must have made a mistake."

Suddenly Karissa could sense his awkwardness.

"I'm sorry to have bothered you, miss. Maybe she meant the neighbor on the other side. But I was sure—"

"Mr. Kelley, I'm Karissa Andrews—*Mrs.* Andrews. My husband died last month—in an accident."

Karissa saw the pain shoot through Holden's eyes. She was immediately sorry and wanted to take back the abrupt explanation. She still had a hard time talking about Michael's death. She had only just met this man; she shouldn't have told him in such a straightforward way. But there really was no other way to say it. She put her hand to her mouth in an effort to conceal her embarrassment.

"I'm sorry, Mrs. Andrews. I had no idea. You're just . . . it's just that you're so . . . I mean, you can't be more than . . ."

"I'm almost twenty." Karissa didn't want him to be sorry for her, or sorry for not realizing she was the widow Mattie had told him about. "Please, don't be sorry. Really. You couldn't have known."

"And I would have never guessed," Holden whispered huskily, seemingly lost in his own thoughts as he looked at her.

"Mr. Kelley, are you all right? You seem—"

"Please, forgive me, Mrs. Andrews. I didn't mean to stare. I . . . I just . . ." Holden stumbled over his words. Trying to regain his composure, he took a deep breath and began again. "Okay. Now, let's get back to the yard. Aunt Mattie's lawn is mowed every week, and I check her fruit trees from time to time. Next week is a good time to fertilize. Would that be okay with you? This is free of charge, you understand."

Karissa shrugged. "I guess so," she answered. She didn't really know anything about yard work. Her father and brother had always taken care of the outside of the Hill home and her mother the inside—except, of course, for a few flowers and tomato plants her mother planted and tended.

"Good. I'll be by tomorrow evening, then, about this time," Holden said. Then he turned abruptly and walked from the yard. Crossing the driveway, he walked directly to Mattie's backyard and entered her back door without knocking.

"Mattie! Where are you?" Karissa could hear Holden's voice boom throughout the entire Sloan house. She heard Mattie's cheerful response to Holden's call but couldn't make out the exact words.

Karissa turned back to her rosebushes. "He says you need pruning. I'm sorry. I won't do it today. He says it can wait. It's so hard—I know. You thought everything was going all right. I understand how you feel. Poor little bush." Karissa stroked the little leaves tenderly and examined more closely the place Holden said a bud was forming. Just as she leaned to have a closer look, she felt the baby kick within her.

She straightened suddenly and stood as still as possible. Holding her hands across her stomach, she felt the tears spring suddenly to her eyes. *It's all right, baby. Everything's going to be all right.* The reality of a living spark of hope leapt as surely within her heart as her unborn child had in her womb.

Wrapping her arms tightly around herself, Karissa stared off into the deep violet blue of the early evening sky. There in the distance, she saw it—the evening star. It couldn't have been a more perfect sky, nor a more perfect star. It couldn't have been a more perfect moment—except she had no one to share it with.

Karissa Hill Andrews was alone in this special moment. The tears spilled over and tumbled down her cheeks. She had never felt so alone in all her life.

———

From Mattie and Ben's screened back porch, Holden watched the beautiful young widow wipe her tears away with the back of her hand. How could life be so cruel? Holden fought back his anger. It was hard enough what he had been through, but this young woman—this was just too much to understand. He wanted to sit with her and let her pour out the pain she must be experiencing. He wanted her to have someone she could lean on, to talk to. No, that wasn't true. He didn't want her to have someone; much to his own surprise, he wanted to *be* that someone. After all, no one knew better than he did what she was feeling and fearing. No one could possibly know the sudden pain of having your heart ripped wide open with such unbelievable news. No one, that is, except Holden. And, he wanted her to know it.

He wanted to reach out to her—he wanted to touch not only her tears but her pain. He felt it with her, and he hadn't felt anything like this—in fact, hadn't felt anything at all—for quite a long time. He didn't exactly know what to do, so he did the only thing he could for now—nothing.

# Ten

"How far along does the doctor say you are?" Kate asked Karissa the next time they talked on the phone.

"I haven't been to a doctor, Mama. I didn't know where to go and then Michael's accident . . ." Karissa suddenly sounded fearful. "Oh, Mama, do you think the baby's okay? I mean, what if it's not? What shall I do? What doctor should I call?"

Kate calmed her daughter and said she'd call back later with the name of a doctor for her, hopefully even an appointment.

"Did you know that Karissa hasn't been seen by a doctor?" Kate was furious when she finally reached Mark Andrews at his office.

"No, I didn't. I'm sorry, Kate. I never thought to ask her about that. Do you know a good one? I don't want her seen by Phyl's doctor. You understand."

"You mean she still doesn't know?"

"She's not been in the best frame of mind. I don't want to make things worse . . ."

"You don't want to upset her? What about Karissa? What about the baby?"

"That's not what I mean. I'm just not sure how she'll react," Mark said. "Or what she'll do. I think it best to give this as much time as possible. Listen, Kate. Make an appointment and take Karissa. Send the bill here to me, okay? To my office, not my home. Understand?"

"I haven't a way to take her, Mark. She won't drive Michael's car and Gerald took ours when he left. You'll have to take her."

"Me? But that's more a mother's job—not a father-in-law's."

"I don't have . . . I can't. And besides, I have the kids."

"Can't you get someone to watch the kids?"

"Sure. But I still don't have a way to get there."

"Okay, tell you what. Make the appointment and I'll drive you and Karissa. Would that work?"

Kate laughed. "You big baby. You don't want to go into the doctor's office, do you?"

"Give me a break, will you? This baby stuff is for women. You're her mother. This is your job!" Mark teased.

"Okay. I'll make the appointment. Dr. Milford is my doctor. In fact, he delivered Karissa. I can trust him to keep his mouth shut. I'll make the appointment for me so his receptionist won't get suspicious, and . . . well, just leave it to me."

"You don't strike me as a devious woman, Kate. This is a side of you I haven't seen."

"You don't know me at all, Mark. In fact . . ." Kate thought better of telling Mark that Gerald was probably thinking the same thing.

---

Gerald Hill had spent the last two weeks in a cheap motel on the edge of town. He had spent long hours in the motel room, praying prayers of repentance and getting the pages of his old-new Bible smudged with tears. When he was sure he had fully repented, then, and only then, would he ask God to help him have the strength to ask Kate's forgiveness. He pictured himself wrapped in her arms, holding her close and giving, not just taking from the love they had shared for more than twenty years.

He called Margie to relay the message to Kate that he wasn't ready to face her yet. He would soon, but not just yet.

"How did he sound, Margie?" Kate had asked.

"Beaten."

"Oh no. I hope I wasn't too hard on him. Maybe I should go to him, you know, just to make sure he's . . ."

"Oh, no you don't. You don't know where he is, and I'm not going to tell you. He made me promise. He's got a lot of thinking to do, Kate. Don't get in God's way. You made your stand, don't you dare waver."

---

The next afternoon Margie stayed with the two measles-patterned Hill children while Kate went with Mark to take Karissa to the doctor. Kate looked forward to the afternoon out, even if it was spent in the doctor's office.

"Afternoon, Mrs. Hill." The stiff, elderly woman at the front desk looked over her glasses at Kate. "I'm surprised to see you here again. I thought that after Lisa . . ." Her voice trailed off and Kate smiled back sweetly.

"It's probably nothing. I'm getting to that age, you know. But if it is—then it's God's will, I guess."

"God, humph. God's got nothing to do with it." Kate could barely make out her mumbled words. "Doctor will be right with you. Miss Karissa, I must say you're looking very well. Sorry to hear about your young husband, though. Such a shame . . . so young . . ." The woman clucked her tongue. "Just never know, do we? One minute full of life . . . the next . . ."

"Good morning, ladies."

Karissa gave the gentle old Dr. Milford a big smile and rushed inside his office, followed by Kate.

"Now, Kate," the doctor said, "what's this all about? Let's see, Lisa is . . ."

"It's not me, Doctor. It's Karissa. I didn't want your old busybody out there to know. Karissa is pregnant."

"Karissa?" Dr. Milford settled his gaze on Karissa. "Are you sure?"

Karissa told him all her symptoms, about her morning sickness and her sleepy afternoons. "After all, I've watched Mama go through this a dozen times."

"Kassy! You've only seen me this way five times. Not a dozen." Kate's face reddened with embarrassment.

"Seems like a dozen to me," Dr. Milford quipped. "Now let's have a look."

Mark was waiting in the car when they walked out of the doctor's office.

"The baby is fine—good, strong heartbeat," Kate said, beaming at Karissa as they got in the car. "The doctor thinks she's about six months along—even though she's small."

"Hey! We're over half done!" Mark teased Karissa.

"What do you mean *we*?" Karissa told Mark everything the doctor had said, including his teasing comments. The doctor had reassured her that soon her nauseous mornings would be behind her—and the rest—"Well," he joked, "that will soon be all out in front!"

"He used that same joke on me when I carried Karissa," Kate laughed. "You'd think he could find a newer one."

"How about an ice cream?" Mark invited.

"I'm tired. Can I just go home and have my nap?" Karissa begged.

"Sure. Whatever you want. That's what you're supposed to say to expectant mothers, right?" He glanced at Kate in the backseat.

"Right." Kate was glad that Michael wasn't here to spoil this day for Kassy. And she felt guilty for being glad.

Mark swerved into Karissa's driveway, then jumped out and ran around to let Karissa out the other side.

"You two coming in?" Karissa asked.

"I really need to get home, Kassy. Lisa has been so fussy. I hate to leave her with Margie a moment longer than necessary."

"Sure, you go on. Thanks for driving, Mark. I can't drive Michael's car."

"It's your car now, Karissa. Remember, we changed the registration into your name."

"I don't know—it still feels like . . ."

"Don't worry about it, honey. You don't want to drive it? Then don't." Kate didn't want Karissa doing anything she didn't want to do.

After dropping Karissa off, Mark suggested they have a cup of coffee at the cafe downtown. "It's only a block or two out of the way, and besides, Lisa may be having the time of her life. You need a break, too."

Kate hesitated, then agreed. She wanted to talk to Mark about Michael's car, anyway. She hoped he would be open to a suggestion. Over a cup of coffee seemed like a good place to discuss it.

---

Phyllis Andrews sat motionless in Irene's car at the end of the block. Her friend had insisted she get out if only for a moment or two. The cafe had been the perfect outing, a small bowl of orange sherbet and a cup of tea—the perfect afternoon refreshment. She had even felt somewhat better—until the moment she saw Mark take Kate's arm and guide her politely into the Summerwind Cafe.

"Take me home, Irene." Phyllis seethed inside. "How dare he squire that low-class woman around town. How long has this been going on, I wonder?"

"Now, Phyl, you don't know that anything's been 'going on.' "

"You saw it too, didn't you? Don't tell me I don't know my own husband's weakness. And don't tell me I don't recognize a two-bit—"

"Phyllis, stop it! You're making a mountain out of a molehill."

"Oh, no I'm not. But just watch me. . . . Mark my words, Irene, I will!"

# Eleven

"How long has this little . . . this little *thing* been going on?" Mark had never seen Phyllis so agitated. Her eyes snapped with excited anger. "How long have you and Kate Hill been—"

"Stop it, Phyllis. You don't know anything."

"I saw you today—with my own eyes. I know what I saw. You and Karissa's mother, of all people."

Mark steeled himself against another of her onslaughts. Usually she needed a martini or two before she threw such a temper. But this time she seemed perfectly sober. Not even a tranquilizer's effect could be noticed.

"You didn't see anything!" Mark said firmly.

"I was downtown with Irene, just when you and your little lady friend walked into the cafe. Are you saying I was hallucinating?"

"No. I am saying you didn't see anything, because there was nothing to see. I simply took Kate for a cup of coffee, that's all. We had to discuss Karissa's . . . well, what to do with Michael's car." Mark wasn't about to tell her of the visit to the doctor.

"You had the nerve to discuss Michael with that woman!"

"*That woman,* as you put it, is Michael's mother-in-law! Karissa's mother. Pull yourself together, Phyllis. We have to discuss the children with the Hills."

"*Was,* Mark, *was* Michael's mother-in-law. Michael is dead now. Isn't that enough? I want that family out of my life! Do you hear me? You stay away from them. I'm telling you, I'll make things so impossible for you—and for her. You so much as tip your hat to her on the street and I promise you—do you hear me?—I promise you I'll make sure everyone in town knows it. Even that young pastor friend of yours! I swear, I'll do it."

"Phyllis! This is vicious, even for you! Let me tell you a thing or two. Michael didn't leave Karissa very well set financially. I don't know what he did with his paycheck. But her household bills were a mess. She had no money, even for groceries. I tell you, you smear the Hills' name and I'll make sure everyone also knows what a lousy job you did as a mother!"

Phyllis and Mark stood facing each other shouting as if they were both deaf.

"How dare you speak to me like that!" Phyllis screamed.

"How dare I not? And shame on me for not speaking like that sooner."

Suddenly Phyllis softened her tone, a sly smile stealing across her face. Reaching for Mark's shirt collar, she tugged gently. "I can't bear the thought that I could lose you, too," she whispered, tipping her face up toward Mark. "I couldn't stand it. I just couldn't stand it." She pulled him close, ran her long fingers around his neck, and pulled him into her kiss. When Mark didn't move or respond, she increased the intensity of her kiss and moved provocatively against him.

Mark closed his eyes and slipped his hands around his wife's slender waist. He hated being used, but it was all he knew: it was Phyllis's best tool of manipulation. He didn't resist her advances. It had been too long; he had been through too much. She was, after all, his wife.

———

"Yes?" Kate answered the knock at her door. A man in work clothes stood with a small toolbox in his hand.

"I'm here to install the phone, ma'am."

"The phone? I think you must have the wrong address."

"Is this the Hill residence?"

"It is."

"Mrs. Hill?"

"Yes."

"I have a work order right here with your name and address on it."

"Let me see that." Kate took the work order and checked it herself. There was no mistake. A phone had been ordered. At the bottom she saw the signature: *Gerald A. Hill.*

"Come in," Kate said, stepping to one side. She stood staring at the paper in her hand. Gerry! It had been a little over two weeks and she hadn't heard anything from him except one impersonal note, and she'd found some money stuck in a milk bottle on the porch last week. It had been enough to keep her and the children in groceries. She had even allowed the children to buy hot lunch at school. They loved it and it saved her from having to carry as many groceries the eight blocks from the A&P.

"Here's your number, Mrs. Hill. It's working fine."

"Thank you so much." Kate still couldn't believe it. For years she and Karissa had been begging for a phone. Gerald had never seen a need for it. In a town this small, with neighbors this close, there was always someone around in case of an emergency. He said his daughter would just find excuses to talk to her friends when she should be doing homework or helping her mother. Kate had finally dropped it, trying to keep peace.

It had been the same when she wanted a radio, although Gerald finally bought a small clock radio for the bedroom. He needed to hear the weather reports in the morning. That justified the radio. He was immovable when it came to a TV set. There would be no television in the Hill household. Kate never told him she often brought the radio down into the kitchen just as soon as he left for work.

She stared at the phone for a moment and nearly jumped out of her skin when it rang. She let it ring twice more, then reached tentatively for the receiver.

"Hello?" she said timidly.

"Kate? It's me, Gerry."

"Gerry?" Kate pulled a kitchen chair toward the phone and sat down before her legs gave out beneath her.

"Do you like the phone?"

"It just came. How did . . . I mean why . . . it's just that I can't understand . . ."

"I've been wrong, Kate. I wanted to tell you how wrong I've been. I wanted to talk to you, to hear your voice. I guess what I'm trying to say is . . . I put myself in your position. I shut myself off—that is, I couldn't reach you. I couldn't stand it. Then I realized, for the first time, what I had done to you. I cut you off from outside contact. I'm so sorry, Kate, for so many things."

"Gerry, it's all right. It's okay."

"No, it's not. I've been thinking—and praying a lot lately. I have a lot yet to do."

"Gerry, I don't know what to say. . . ."

"You don't have to say anything. Just listen. Can I call you sometime? I mean . . . I love you . . . I can't stand not being able to hear your voice."

"Gerry, we need to talk."

"I know. That's why I put in the phone."

"I mean, really talk. Do we need a phone for that?"

"I didn't think you'd want to see me."

"Gerry Hill, we've been married twenty-one years. I haven't wanted to see our marriage come to an end. I've been hoping we could somehow work things out."

"Kate, listen to me. I'm not very good at this—but, would you go out with me Saturday night?"

"What?"

"I mean it. Can you get Karissa to watch the kids? Or how about Jodie? She's old enough to leave them with, isn't she? She's almost sixteen, for goodness' sake. Can't she stay with the kids?"

"Yes, of course she can. She helps out all the time." Kate could hardly believe what she was hearing. Her own husband was asking to take her out on a date. "Gerry, what's this all about?"

"I—we need some time to ourselves. We need to be together, or rather, I need to be with you, alone. Is that an unreasonable thing to ask? I mean, maybe you don't want to see—"

"It's a date!" Kate interrupted. "Be here at seven." Kate paused then added, "Gerry?"

"Yes?"

"The same rules apply as before."

"Rules?"

"Don't be late; don't honk the horn; come to the door like a gentleman. But there's one thing more."

"What's that? I'll do anything."

"This time you have to face my children, not my father."

"Do they hate me, Kate?"

"No, Gerry, they don't hate you. They're hurt right now. I can't fix that . . . only you can do that."

"I'll do my best, Kate. I may need some time, though. Can you give me time?"

"I've given you twenty-one years. I guess I can give you a few more." Kate smiled into the phone.

"Will you take my number and call me if you need anything?"

Kate wrote the number Gerry gave her on the back of an envelope she found close by.

"Gerry, I'm sorry . . ."

"Don't be sorry, Kate. Don't you ever be sorry for anything. I'm glad this happened."

"You are?"

"We'll talk more Saturday night, okay?"

"Saturday night, then."

After a brief, awkward silence he said, "You don't have to say anything, Kate. It's good just to hear you breathe."

Kate laughed, not understanding what had happened to her husband but hoping there was still a chance for them, a chance to start over.

"Will you call again?" she asked.

"Probably. But not until after Saturday night, okay? I'm working through some things. It's taking a bit longer than I'd like, but . . ."

"Take all the time you need, Gerry. There's no rush on this end."

"Karissa? How's she doing?"

"Fine." Kate didn't want to tell Gerry about the baby just yet. "She's doing just fine. Sandy's staying with her. I call her from Margie's every day or so."

"Call her now and give her your number. She needs to know she can call whenever she might need to talk." Gerry sounded almost defeated, or was it tired? Kate would be glad to finally see his face. She could tell so much just by looking at her husband.

"I'll say good-night, my darling." Gerry's voice was thick with emotion. Kate couldn't remember ever hearing Gerry use a term of endearment toward her. Was it because the phone gave him enough distance that he felt safe? Or was it because he couldn't reach her with his arms and hands that he needed to say it? It didn't really matter; Kate loved hearing it.

"Say it again, will you?"

"Say what, good-night? Or, my darling?"

"That . . . last part."

"My precious darling."

Kate closed her eyes tight, squeezing the tears out and down her cheeks. "Gerry, I . . ."

"I'll see you Saturday night. And, Kate, wear that pretty pink dress you wore to Karissa's wedding reception, will you?"

"I guess I can . . ."

"Good, see you then." Gerry hung up the phone quickly. Kate stood looking at the receiver in disbelief. She held one miracle in her hand and another in her heart. She hung up the phone and, without lifting her hand from it, covered her face with her other hand and wept. Edie and Lisa stood wide-eyed and silent, watching their mother. As young as they were, they knew enough to let her have her moment—her miracle moment.

---

Across town, Mark lay spent, with his wife snuggled tight against him. "Mark, sweetheart," Phyllis began sweetly, "I've been thinking."

"Oh no. Now what?"

"Don't spoil it, Mark. You're not the only one who's concerned about Karissa."

"I'll bet." Mark wasn't easily persuaded.

"Don't be like that," Phyllis teased. "I have a heart, too. Haven't I just proved that to you? Do you need me to prove it again. . . ?" She traced Mark's ear with a perfectly manicured fingernail.

"No." Mark swatted her hand away.

"I've been so involved with my own grief for Michael, so deep in my own pain, that I haven't been able to reach out to Karissa. How's she doing? I mean, how's she really doing?"

"She's getting better." Did Mark dare tell her the bruises on her face were gone, that Karissa's ankle was finally its normal size again? Did she need to know that Michael's beating had left Karissa broken-hearted and ridden with guilt for carrying his baby? Phyllis's only grandchild? No. He wouldn't tell her. Not yet.

"I'm glad to hear that. Maybe I should have a talk with her about the trust fund. Do you think it's time I did that?"

"You? Why you?"

"Because, my darling, I'm the administrator of the fund. Have you forgotten?"

Mark hadn't forgotten. He had been reminded ever so coolly of that fact several weeks ago at the bank. Though his own father had set up the fund, Mark had turned over the management of it to Phyllis years ago. Their son had been so unreasonably demanding, yet Phyllis had always taken Michael's side.

Mark had finally given in to the pressure and made her the administrator, taking his name off the fund completely. He wanted nothing more to do with the wholesale spoiling of his only child. He figured as soon as the money was gone, Phyllis would be out of control, and Michael would have to learn financial lessons the hard way. He dreaded the day but knew the sooner it came the better.

Besides, Phyllis had always been a good money manager. She did wonders decorating their own home on the money Mark allotted to her for such projects. And there was Michael's car. She had managed to get that for him for graduation. Not every boy in the class of '55 drove a car like Michael's Crown Victoria—a fact that first caused Mark a measure of discomfort, but that he got over when he saw Michael's face the day he drove it home.

"How much is in the fund?" Mark asked.

"I'm not sure," Phyllis said. "The principal remains the same. The interest fluctuates. I paid Michael's allowance out of the interest." She snuggled closer to Mark and said, "But don't you worry about it, darling. I'll take care of everything. I'll speak to Karissa first thing in the morning. It's time I saw her anyway. It's just that it's been too painful for me."

"And what about her?" Once again Mark felt the anger rising within him, along with the self-contempt he often felt after being used by his wife. "What about Karissa, don't you think this has been painful for her, too?"

"I'm just trying to get you to see my pain. You've been so concerned about her, you haven't even noticed me," Phyllis whined.

"She's helpless; you're not." Mark knew it was an understatement. "You can take care of yourself; she can't."

"And her mother, is she helpless too?"

Mark pulled away from Phyllis and got out of bed. "Let's leave her mother out of this."

"You stay away from her, and I will. But I meant what I said. You see her again, and I'll make sure—"

"I heard you. And I warn you, you leave Kate Hill alone."

"Then *you* leave Kate Hill alone!" Phyllis's voice was laced with threat.

Fifteen minutes later, Mark slammed out of the house, grabbing his jacket on the way. Driving around in the dark, peaceful little town, Mark thought of going to the small, dimly lit bar downtown. They were open late, and he knew he'd find a friendly face or warm conversation there. Instead he headed for the all-night diner out on the edge of town. He'd have a cup of coffee, then he'd stop by his office and work. He'd have more time for Karissa that way anyway.

————————

Phyllis climbed into a steaming hot bubble bath to calm her nerves. She really didn't enjoy deceiving her husband—there just wasn't any other way. She knew exactly how much was in that trust fund, but there was no good reason to divulge that information to Mark. And it would only upset Mark to know about the personal loans she had taken using the trust fund as security. Since Michael's death, the bank had called twice and reported that they would need to take the loan payments out of the interest since Phyllis had missed the last two months. It didn't matter to Phyllis. Michael was no longer here to demand his monthly allowance, so it seemed the easiest way. There certainly wasn't any need to tell her husband.

Besides, Phyllis had made herself the beneficiary should anything happen to Michael. Mark didn't need to know that either. Phyllis was determined that Karissa would never get her hands on that money. Now if Michael had ever had a child—well, that would have been a different story. But now that would never happen.

# Twelve

Sitting alone in a booth near the back of the diner, Mark didn't see Holden Kelley come in.

"Hey, Mr. Andrews, good to see you. Mind if I sit down?"

"Kelley. Please, join me."

"How's it goin'? The Lugonia Avenue project coming along all right?"

"Yeah, just some last-minute glitches with the water department. Nothing unusual. We'll be ready for you to begin within a week or so."

Holden Kelley was the best landscape architect in the entire valley. He was even in demand in the city, but Holden preferred working in his small native community. He had made quite a name for himself with his beautiful artistic designs, landscaping the most prestigious model homes and even a few commercial buildings.

"How's the park project coming?" Mark inquired. "I hear you're donating all your own efforts; quite a generous thing to do, Kelley."

"Not pure generosity, Mr. Andrews. It's good promotion, too. Besides, this is my hometown. Not many people can say that, you know. Most everyone you meet these days came here from somewhere else."

"You're right about that. How is the work coming along?"

"Rather well, I must say. Working with the city employees has been a challenge, though. They've been taught mainly mowing and weeding—they're not really up on developing and maintaining healthy plants and shrubs."

"City Hall looks great."

"Thanks. That's my one trophy piece. Even I like it."

"You usually don't?"

"No one is more critical of my work than I am. That's for sure. My wife said it more than once. She was right, too."

"I'm sorry, I didn't know you were married."

"A long time ago. Maybe not so long. It seems a lifetime ago."

"What happened?" Mark was surprised at his own intrusive question.

"She died. Killed in a car accident. She and my little boy. He was not quite two."

"I didn't know that. I'm sorry, I didn't mean to—"

"It's okay. I guess you've been going through a pretty rough time yourself."

"Yeah, it's been tough. I guess time will make a difference. I just keep telling myself that anyway." Mark liked Holden Kelley. He saw a quality of work and ethics in him that he didn't find in many of the other subcontractors he hired. Karissa's father was the only other one he could even think of offhand. "I have a daughter-in-law, though. I want to get to know her better. I guess we all got off to a rough start when the kids ran off and got married. I don't want to lose her, too."

"Got to be hard on her," Holden said, sipping his coffee.

"Yeah, it has been." *In more ways than you can imagine,* Mark thought. "Say, you could give me a hand, if you'd be willing."

"What's that?"

"Can you send a crew over and take care of her

yard on a regular basis? I don't know if you even do residential maintenance, but I'd sure be glad to add your men to my payroll."

"Where does she live? I can go have a look."

Mark wrote down Karissa's address on the back of his business card and handed it to Holden.

"Well, I'll be . . . I've already met your daughter-in-law, Mr. Andrews. I just didn't make the connection . . . until now. She lives right next door to my aunt."

"The Sloans? They're relatives of yours?"

Holden nodded and sipped his coffee.

"Isn't that something! Karissa lives right next door!"

"Now, that *is* something," Holden remarked with a cryptic smile. "I already do my aunt's yard and she asked me to help out Mrs. Andrews, too. Said I'd be glad to. Plan to start tomorrow, as a matter of fact."

"That's great! Small world, isn't it? I'd like to be the one to pay you for this, Holden. I really appreciate it."

"No need, really. I'm glad to do it as a favor."

"No, no . . . I insist, Holden. I'm sure glad I ran into you. Couldn't sleep. Too much on my mind, I guess," Mark said.

"Know what you mean." Holden ran his finger across his short blond crew cut. "I was having a little trouble with that myself last night."

———

"I'm sorry to call so late, Mama. Were you upstairs?"

Kate wasn't upstairs. She was in the kitchen making herself a cup of hot milk, hoping it would help her relax.

"We've called each other six times since the phone was put in! In one day we've talked more than we have in a year!" Kate laughed into the phone. "Isn't it wonderful? I can't believe it yet."

"You know, Mama, I feel so alone sometimes . . ."

"Kassy . . ."

"But now with the phone, I can just call you. I don't feel so alone anymore."

Kate wondered if Gerald knew just how much Karissa appreciated the phone. She would tell him when she saw him Saturday night. "I'll tell your dad how much this means to you, honey. He'll be glad to hear it."

"Have you heard from him?"

"Oh yes. Didn't I tell you?"

"Tell me what? No, you didn't tell me anything."

"I have a date Saturday night."

"What?"

"A date. Your father called me half an hour after the phone was in. He asked me to go out with him Saturday night."

"Really?"

"He asked me to wear the pink dress I wore . . ." Kate stopped midsentence.

"Oh, Mama, you look wonderful in that dress. See, he did notice. You thought he didn't!" Karissa's tone spoke of her delighted excitement for her mother.

"Where do you suppose he will take me?"

"I don't know, maybe the country club?"

"I hardly think so, Kassy. Your dad sounds like he's changed all right, but I'm not expecting the country club. Even I wouldn't be comfortable there."

"Wait a minute, Mama. There's someone at the door." Karissa laid the phone down before Kate could stop her. In a minute she was back and sounded excited. "It's Mark, Mama. He just stopped by on his way to work to see if I was okay. Here, say something to him."

"Hello there," Mark said quietly.

"Hi, yourself. Isn't it amazing? Karissa and I can talk a dozen times a day if we want to."

"Welcome to the twentieth century, Kate." He laughed.

"Thanks. Better go now. Put Kassy back on, will you?"

"Yeah, I will. See you soon—I'll call you tomorrow! Isn't this great?"

Mark handed the phone back to Karissa, walked across the kitchen, and watched the young woman as she said good-night to her mother. "And, how did this happen?" Mark asked his beaming daughter-in-law.

"My dad put it in."

"You're kidding."

"Will wonders never cease?" Karissa's eyes sparkled with excitement. "Guess what else?"

"I can't guess. Just tell me."

"The baby is really starting to move a lot now."

"No kidding?" Mark couldn't help but join in her excitement.

"No kidding." Karissa's eyes filled with tears. "I guess Pastor Jim knew what he was talking about after all."

"Pastor Jim?"

"Yeah. Remember what he said at the funeral about a door of hope? Well, if this baby's a girl, I'm thinking about naming her Hope."

Suddenly, naming the baby made him or her seem more real to Mark than ever. If Phyllis only knew!

"Karissa, I have something to tell you now. I'm afraid it might take the excitement off this moment, but it can't be helped."

"What's wrong?" Karissa sat heavily in a kitchen chair.

"Phyllis wants to come and see you. She's the administrator of Michael's trust fund. I have tried to change it. But without her signature, I can't do anything about it. It's a mistake I made several years ago, putting her in charge of it in the first place. But it's done now. Anyway, she said she will be coming over in the morning to discuss it with you. She'll explain about the income from it and all."

"But I thought you said—"

"I've been putting money into your account regularly. I would continue if necessary. But Michael's trust will provide you a modest but adequate amount each month. You're a good money manager. There should be plenty for routine expenses. If you need anything more, just let me know."

"Tomorrow? She's coming tomorrow?" Karissa didn't look too excited about having to face her mother-in-law. "Does she know about the baby?"

"I haven't told her. I'm not sure it's a good idea yet, but we can't hide it much longer, can we?" Mark glanced at Karissa's tummy.

"No, we can't. At least, *I* can't. I'm getting bigger every day. I'll just have to keep my bathrobe on for her visit. It's big enough to hide my stomach a little while longer."

"Just get through the morning as best you can. Ask her whatever questions you have. You can also ask me later, if you want." Mark kissed the top of Karissa's head. "I wish you didn't have to deal with her at all. However, it can't be helped. I'm sorry."

"I'll be okay."

"I know you will," Mark assured her.

As he closed the door and walked toward his car he said quietly to himself, "I certainly *hope* she'll be okay."

# Thirteen

Karissa wasn't prepared for the news Phyllis's visit brought. Michael's trust fund was almost completely depleted. The down payment on the house, Michael's car, and his large monthly allowance had eaten away large chunks of the trust's principal.

"I don't understand," Karissa said. "Mark told me that there was plenty of money to—"

"There was, dear. But you see, then Michael needed a car, and his college tuition, and of course this house. The funeral alone was several thousand dollars. Well, I'm sure you can see that all was very expensive. His paycheck was what paid the bills, Karissa. Surely even you know that."

Karissa couldn't comprehend all that Phyllis was telling her. But she had no reason to disbelieve her mother-in-law; she sounded so knowledgeable and businesslike. "I guess I just didn't know . . ." Karissa said.

"Of course you didn't. How could you?" Phyllis patted Karissa's hand condescendingly.

"I mean I just thought—"

"That there was money here? Money for you? I'm afraid not, my dear. It's all tied up in assets. And, what's more, I'm afraid that Michael's car will have to be transferred back into my name so that, if we have to, we can sell it. I'm also the administrator of Michael's estate. It's perfectly in order. Here are the title transfer forms. You just sign here and I'll take care of the rest."

"I'll need the money, won't I?" Karissa asked absently.

"You'll need money from somewhere—that's for sure."

"I don't understand. I just thought—"

"No one expects you to understand about these things, Karissa. Surely Michael would have told you if he thought you would have understood. I'm sure he wanted to include you in such matters. However, some people just don't have the background for understanding . . ."

Karissa felt a wave of nausea coming over her as Phyllis rattled on. She fought to maintain her composure and focus her attention back on what her mother-in-law was saying.

"Where are Michael's things?" Phyllis demanded. "Have you gotten rid of his clothes and such?"

"No. They're in the garage. I packed them and put them out there."

"I see. Well, if you don't mind, then, I'll be taking them home with me. Now, if you'll just sign the transfer, I'll be back later to take the car. I'll have it washed and gone over by the mechanic before I put it up for sale."

Karissa hesitated. Nothing was going the way Mark predicted. He said there was a generous amount in Michael's trust fund. It wasn't for her; it was for the baby. How could she support the baby? She couldn't get a job now—not six months pregnant.

"You know, Karissa, Mark would be heartbroken if he knew how Michael had squandered the money. He couldn't handle the money in the first place. That's why Mark gave it to me to take care of. Michael's death has been especially hard on him. I would hate to think what this would do to him."

"But he's been here . . . I've seen him. He seems to be handling it very well."

"I see him in the middle of the night, Karissa. I'm his wife—I know. I've heard him sobbing when he thinks no one knows. He's being strong for you, my dear. This has almost sent him over the edge. I'm afraid that I've not only lost my only son but am near losing my husband, too." Phyllis dabbed at her eyes. "No one knows how hard it is to lose a child. And when it's your only son—it's unspeakable pain. Just unspeakable. Someday, if you ever have a child of your own, then you'll understand a mother's feelings."

Feeling drained and weak, Karissa stood and motioned Phyllis toward the back door. "They're out in the garage. Let me show you." Leading the way out into the yard, Karissa felt awkward in her robe but was glad she had left it on to hide her pregnancy from Phyllis. Whatever else came of this morning, she certainly wasn't going to tell her about the baby today. Not until she figured out her financial situation. Certainly not before she could talk to her mother or to Mark.

Inside the garage, Phyllis turned to Karissa. "You look a little peaked, Karissa. I can handle this. Why don't you go back in the house and lie down. I'll take care of this. It's difficult, I know. But once I have his things out of here, you won't have to look at them anymore. That will make it better, I promise."

"I haven't—" Karissa stopped. She didn't need to tell Phyllis that she hadn't been in the garage since Mark parked the car inside, out of sight. There was no reason to go in the garage once Michael's things had been packed.

"Go on, now. Perhaps you should make yourself a cup of tea first, then lie down. Honestly, I can take it from here."

Karissa turned and went back into the kitchen, grateful to be finished with her discussion with Phyllis. She looked at the phone and wanted to call her mother or Mark. Instead, she went toward the bathroom. Falling across the toilet, she let the sobs she had fought to control find their way to the surface.

———

As soon as she knew Karissa was safely in the house, Phyllis ripped into the boxes containing Michael's things. Her pain at seeing his sweaters, jeans, and tennis shoes was pushed aside in her desperate need to find the small metal box containing his important papers. As soon as possible, she needed to get them into her possession, perhaps even into a security box at the bank.

Phyllis had felt unnerved in the kitchen when she'd noticed Karissa resting her hand on her stomach—after she'd talked about losing her only son. Karissa *did* look a little heavier—and pale, as if she weren't feeling very well. If Karissa was indeed carrying Michael's child, then she needed to get this business taken care of quickly!

Seeing the small metal container at the bottom of one of the boxes, Phyllis breathed a sigh of relief. Repacking the sweaters carefully around it, she picked up the box and headed for the car. She would gather the rest of his things another time. The metal box was all she needed for now. After she got home she would take to the bank whatever papers she needed to conceal for safekeeping.

———

Within minutes of hearing her daughter's fear-filled voice, Kate asked Ned Smith to drive her over to Karissa's. Margie offered to stay with the children and fix them some supper while Kate handled the situation with Karissa.

"Mama, what am I going to do? I thought everything was going to be okay. Mark said—"

"I know what Mark said. But, he obviously didn't have all the facts. I wonder what he'd say now?"

"I don't know."

"Have you called him?"

"I tried. He's out at a job site. I can't get to him until later tonight. His secretary said she'd leave a message for him. She didn't know if he'd be back to the office tonight or not." Karissa wrapped her arms tightly around her mother and buried her face in Kate's neck. "Oh, Mama, I'm so scared."

"There's nothing to be scared about, Kassy. You have your house, don't you? Isn't it paid for?"

"I think so, but it's the Andrewses' money that paid for it. It's not mine."

"Where are the papers, honey? You know, all the insurance papers, the deed—all that stuff. We put it somewhere when we packed Michael's things."

"They're in the garage. I put them in a shoe box on a shelf in the back. Michael used to keep them in a little metal box, but they were getting crushed in there. I took them out and put all his report cards in the metal box and put the papers in the shoe box."

"Let's have a look. I'm not the one who knows about these things. Your father might have a better idea than I do."

Karissa led the way to the garage with Kate close behind.

"What happened here?" Kate asked when Karissa switched on the light.

"Phyllis happened here." Karissa wandered over to the boxes, now open and obviously rummaged through. "She wanted Michael's things, but I guess she changed her mind. Maybe it was too much for her. Maybe it hurt too much."

"Or maybe she was looking for something." Kate

began straightening up the mess. "Wasn't there one more big box?"

"I guess she took that. Maybe it was all she could handle in one day. There's the shoe box." Karissa pointed to a shelf above Kate's head.

They headed back to the kitchen with the box and sat down at the table, trying to make sense of the papers.

"I wish your father could take a look at these." Kate had been as protected as Karissa about insurance policies and the like. She had left that all up to Gerry. He took care of all the finances and business matters. All she had to do was take care of the children and the house. She was beginning to realize what a mistake that had been. A woman never knew when she'd need to understand more than recipes and dress patterns.

"You want to take them with you?" Karissa said. "You'll be seeing him Saturday night. Maybe you could—"

"I think you should call Mark again." Kate realized that Gerry might not be ready to discuss financial dealings with the Andrews family.

———

Upon his arrival, Mark took a place at the kitchen table. Kate and Karissa sat opposite him and told him of Phyllis's visit and her dismal portrayal of Karissa's financial picture.

"That can't be right. I signed with Michael on the mortgage myself. It's paid up now because we put mortgage insurance on the house. I turned in that policy the week after his accident. The down payment didn't come out of his trust fund. Neither did his car. Phyllis paid for that herself . . ." Mark paused. "At least I think she did."

Kate got up and opened the refrigerator to fix

lunch for the three to eat as they examined Michael's papers.

"This can't be right," Mark went on. "Look here, this is a statement of earnings on the trust fund. See? There's plenty of income. What did she say again?"

"She said there wasn't any money left after putting the down payment on the house and buying the car. She said something about tuition and—"

"I paid Michael's tuition," Mark said flatly. "I wonder what she's up to. Look, Karissa, here is a life insurance policy. We started paying that as soon as Michael entered kindergarten. We should turn that in. There's money right here. All we need is a copy of the death certificate. You have that? Good. See here? Here's the benefit amount and right here's your name . . ." Mark couldn't believe his eyes. Michael's insurance was never amended to change the beneficiary from Phyllis to Karissa. "I don't understand—I specifically told Michael to change this. I recall it clearly. He told me it was all taken care of."

"He lied." Kate turned from the counter where she was fixing lunch. "He didn't take care of it, did he?" Mark saw the pain and anger in her eyes.

"Kate, I'm sorry. I had no idea. He said he took care of it, and I believed him."

"We all believed him. When he said he loved Kassy, we believed him. When he said he would protect and love her, we believed him. When he said he would take care of her, we believed him. No, I take that back. I believed him. Gerry didn't, though. He didn't believe him for a moment!"

"Stop it, Mama. I believed him too. I'm the one who was wrong. Not you, not Daddy. Please, Mama . . ." Karissa's sobs came from deep within, and Mark and Kate reached her at the same time. Wrapping their arms around her, they comforted each other as much as they comforted her.

"Look. There is a way out of all this. There may not be much money here, but there's something. You still have the house and I can—"

"No, you can't," Karissa said. "Maybe Michael didn't take his responsibility, but you can't make up for him. You can't support two households."

Mark knew she was right. Much of his own money was tied up in the business. Construction was a risky business. You put in all you had, more than once, hoping the houses would sell before you ran out. If it hadn't been for Phyllis's handling of their household account, they probably would have nothing to show for all Mark's hard work. Then it hit him.

"She hasn't been living on my income. She's been living off Michael's!" Mark suddenly felt ill. "That's it! She's done enough damage. Let me see the rest of the papers in that box."

From beneath all the other statements and various papers, Mark pulled out a folder filled with loan documents. "Did you and Michael get a loan of some kind?"

"Not that I know of."

"You've never signed any papers at the bank, or an application of any sort?"

"No, never."

Mark took a quick look over the approved loan application he held in his hand as the realization began to sink in. Phyllis had borrowed against the principal in Michael's trust fund. In order to do that, the bank had been named beneficiary. The balance of the loan would be paid to the bank in the event of Michael's death. The excess amount, should there be any, would be paid—not to Karissa but to Phyllis. Mark stood slowly, letting the entire understanding of what Phyllis had done sweep over him. He could feel his whole body begin to tremble, and he fought to maintain control.

He thought she had spent her entire life spoiling Michael, when really she had simply used him—used him as she had Mark, and would Karissa if given the opportunity. He was not about to give her that opportunity. He could, in fact, do something to stop her. He would find a way, and he would do it without delay.

"There's one more thing." Kate's voice jerked him back from his thoughts.

"Oh?"

"Karissa, tell him about the car."

"What about the car?"

"Phyllis wants me to sign this transfer form so she can sell it."

"Sell it? Why on earth would she sell it?"

"Mark, calm down. Please, sit down." Kate's voice was soothing and calm. Mark responded and sat down.

"She said," Karissa spoke softly, "that if we had to, we could sell the car. You know, for money, because I don't have any."

"I told you that was not going to—"

"Mark, please. Kassy is just telling you what Phyllis said. Go on, dear."

"She said she was the administrator of Michael's estate and that she might have to sell the car, and having the transfer signed would make it easier."

"Right. It sure would. Tell you what. You go ahead and sign those transfer papers. But not to Phyllis. We're putting the car in your name, Karissa, *and* mine. That way the car can't be sold without both our signatures."

"Or," Kate said quietly, "in your name only. Then you could dispose of the car any way you wanted, right?"

"Right." Mark searched Kate's face for an explanation. Kate raised her eyebrows and Mark finally remembered the conversation they had over coffee after taking Karissa to the doctor. "Oh yes. Right." Mark turned to Karissa. "Do you trust me, Kassy?"

"Of course."

"Then listen to me carefully. Sign the transfer papers and give me the keys to Michael's car. Your mother and I will take it and park it somewhere else. Don't ask any questions, and don't answer any, either. Is that clear?"

"Now, Karissa, I must get back home. Mark, would you be so kind as to drop me off?"

"I'd be glad to. Do you drive, Kate?"

"Yes, I do."

"Good, then you take my car home." Mark handed her the keys. "I'll be taking Michael's car with me. I can drop by later and pick up my car. Just leave the keys under the floor mat. I won't even have to bother you, just in case it's late."

"Isn't that dangerous? Leaving the keys in the car?"

"You're right. I have an extra set at the office. Just push the button and close the door. Lock the keys in the car, or if you'd rather, I can get them later." Mark turned to Karissa. "Is Mattie home this afternoon?"

"I think so, why?"

"I want you to go over there and stay there. Get a few things together and stay the night. Would that be all right with her?"

"She'd love it. Ben hasn't been feeling too well lately and she's been sort of cooped up. I'll go now."

"Good, call Sandy at work the minute you get home, Kate. Tell her not to come back here tonight. Tell her to go to her mother's. I'd rather the girls not be here if—or when—Phyllis returns."

"You think she'll be back?" Karissa asked.

"When she discovers she doesn't have those papers, she will." Mark scooped the papers together and put them back in the shoe box. "Let's put these somewhere safe, shall we? I have a safe at the office. Phyllis doesn't have the combination."

"What are you going to do, Mark?"

"I have my work cut out for me. I'll need to see a lawyer first thing in the morning if I can't get an appointment this afternoon."

# Fourteen

Only too happy to have Karissa stay overnight with her and Ben, Mattie immediately began fixing a full-sized supper. She so seldom had the opportunity to cook for anyone that she seized the chance to "have a celebration."

Karissa found the daybed far too inviting, and when she could no longer resist, she lay down and fell asleep almost immediately. She didn't even hear the lawn mower start up or Holden come in and call for his aunt Mattie.

"Shush, Holden!" Mattie scolded her nephew. "We have a sleeping beauty in the TV room." Holden adored Mattie. She had been almost a mother to him ever since his own passed away when he was seventeen.

"Is that right?" Holden peeked in the doorway and caught sight of Karissa sleeping peacefully on the daybed, with Ben dozing comfortably in the big recliner nearby. The elderly couple spent much of their mornings in the TV room—really a small bedroom on the main floor of the house—watching TV quiz shows and speculating on the answers and what they would do with the money had they been the winners.

"When I checked next door, I didn't see her at the house. I thought she might be away or something."

"She's staying the night. Her family asked if she could be here tonight. Some problem with her mother-in-law, I think."

"So you're hiding her?"

"I guess you could say that. Nobody'd even think to look right next door," Mattie chuckled. "I'm fixing pot roast for supper. You'll stay, won't you?"

"I don't know, Auntie. I'm not cleaned up or anything. Maybe I'd better not."

"I think maybe you'd better. The pot roast is far too much for the three of us. And, besides, well . . . just put it this way, I've already set your place on the table. You wouldn't want me to go to all that work for nothing, now, would you?"

"Guess you've got me there. I wouldn't want you mad at me."

"Good, then it's settled. Now you go on and wash up. Dinner's in half an hour."

After washing up, Holden went out back and began hosing down Mattie's back walkway. A strange car pulling into Karissa's drive caught his attention. He stepped back behind the screened porch and waited. He could see the woman, but she obviously didn't see him.

Holden watched as Phyllis Andrews knocked lightly on Karissa's back door. When no one answered, she tried the locked door and knocked again, a little louder. Looking around, Phyllis walked to the garage and tried to open the large door, then the smaller one on the side. She couldn't manage to get either open and tried to see through the small window in the side door. Squinting, she held her hand against the glass and tried to see inside.

Holden decided to make himself conspicuous. "Help you with something, lady?"

Phyllis turned and immediately spread her lips in a broad, open smile. "Why, yes. I was hoping to find Karissa Andrews. Do you know her?"

"I've met her."

"I see. Isn't she home?"

"Didn't anyone answer the door?"

"No. I don't understand it. She is usually home. Where would she go?"

"Can't say."

"Are you her neighbor?"

"Not exactly. I'm the gardener hereabouts. I look after these two yards. Mr. Andrews hired me."

"The gardener. Strange . . . he didn't mention that to me."

"And would he?"

"Pardon?"

"Mention something so . . . well, you know . . . insignificant."

Not answering Holden's last remark, Phyllis held her hand up to shade her eyes. She scanned the yard again, looked toward the garage, then walked back toward her car. Just before getting in, she said, "If you see Karissa, would you tell her Phyllis was here?"

"If I see her, I might. Will she know who you are?"

"Yes, of course."

"And who might that be?"

"Phyllis Andrews." Phyllis seemed insulted by his questions.

"You a relative, then?"

"I'm her mother-in-law." Phyllis was clearly getting angry now.

"That's hard to believe."

"What?!" Phyllis's lips were drawn tight in an angry pout.

"You look too young to be anyone's mother-in-law." Holden flashed a bright smile. He couldn't miss the sudden change in Phyllis Andrews' demeanor as she looked him up and down with an appreciative gaze.

"Why, are you flirting with me Mr.—Mr. Gardener?" Her sudden-sweetening tone turned Holden's stomach.

"Of course not, ma'am. Just bein' friendly, that's all."

Phyllis turned to open her car door and glanced teasingly over her shoulder. Standing at the back gate, Holden watched her examine her lipstick in her rearview mirror before she smiled at him and backed out of Karissa's driveway.

"Were you flirting with that woman?" Mattie asked disgustedly.

"No, Mattie, I wasn't. But you yourself told me many times, a bee comes quicker to honey than vinegar. How else was I to find out what she was up to?"

Karissa appeared sleepily at the doorway. "Was that Phyllis's car? What was she doing here?"

Holden was startled by Karissa's sudden appearance. "Why, she was just . . . just looking for—"

"Don't you worry about her, now," Mattie interrupted. "It's time to eat." She directed Holden and Karissa back inside and pulled the dining room shade as they sat down to eat.

"God, our heavenly Father," Ben began in his halting but gentle voice, "we thank you for the bountiful provisions you keep blessing us with from day to day. We thank you for these youngsters here with us tonight at our table. Lord, bless them, keep them, and show them your perfect will. In Christ's name, we pray. Amen."

Throughout the meal, Holden kept glancing at Karissa, at her beautiful honey blond hair cascading over her shoulders, and at her warm smile. As she joined in the happy dinnertime chatter, it was obvious to Holden that she loved this older couple and felt perfectly at home with them.

"Now, children," Mattie said once they finished eating, "you go on out back and sit in the cool air. It's a might stuffy in here, if you ask me. I'll just clear up these dishes and—"

"You'll do no such thing. I'll do the dishes," Karissa insisted.

"I'll help." Holden stood to his feet and started picking up the dishes.

"My, my. Looks like you're stuck with me, old lady." Ben smiled at his wife. "You could do worse, you know." He winked at Karissa.

"And I almost did, too," Mattie said. "I'm sure glad I said no to the wrong man and yes to the right one."

Karissa closed her eyes tight and hurried to the kitchen with a stack of dishes. Her sudden, pained expression spoke volumes to Holden, who followed behind with another stack of plates. He pushed through the swinging door and saw her already standing at the sink, her hands plunged deep in the soapy water. She jumped when Holden reached from behind her to pull the window shade down over the sink.

"If you're hiding here, you shouldn't stand in front of a window," he said. "I didn't mean to scare you."

"You didn't."

"You jumped."

"I'm sorry."

"Sorry? For what?"

"For jumping, I guess."

"Karissa Andrews, I . . . ."

Karissa turned to look into Holden's eyes.

"I don't want you to ever be sorry again," he said softly.

"I don't understand."

"I don't either." Holden reached for a clean tea towel and began to wipe the wet dishes. Stacking them carefully on the counter, he watched Karissa as she rinsed the dishes and placed them in the rack for him to dry.

"How did you meet your husband?"

"In high school. I was part of the pep squad, he

was on the football team. It was the thing to do."

"Was he in your graduating class?"

"No, he graduated in '55—two years ahead of me. It was quite a thing for a sophomore to go with a senior. I wasn't his only girlfriend back then. It wasn't until last year, when I was a senior, that we really got serious about each other."

Holden listened intently as he continued to dry and stack the clean dishes.

"I was homecoming queen. Michael was so proud of me that night. He was allowed to go to the dance because he was an alumnus and, of course, a former football player. He made a big deal of being my date that night." Karissa moved away from Holden's side and began wiping off the stove and counters.

"We went steady for a few weeks and everything seemed fine. I really enjoyed being with him—he treated me like *his* queen. Then he started pressuring me. You know, to have our relationship go further. I wanted to wait." Karissa turned her back to Holden and took a deep breath. "He said we needed to get married . . . right away. I couldn't stand to see him unhappy, so on the prom night in January we went across the border to Arizona and got married. Lots of kids did it."

Karissa turned back around and shrugged her shoulders. *Almost as if to apologize,* Holden thought.

"How did your parents take it?"

"They didn't know at first."

"How come?"

"We kept it a secret. Michael said it'd ruin everything if we told them too soon. He needed to prepare his mother. He was worried about getting his money. I didn't care, though. I thought he could get a job."

"And he didn't want to do that?"

"He wanted his dad to give him a job. But he didn't work very hard at it."

"The boss's son, huh?"

"Yeah, no one wanted him on their work crew. He didn't work very hard. I guess he thought he did. He celebrated every Friday night when he got his check."

"And you, did you celebrate?"

"No," Karissa said quietly, "I didn't."

"What happened the night he died?"

"What do you mean?"

"Was he out celebrating that night?"

"Not really. We had a real bad fight"—Karissa's voice dropped to barely above a whisper—"about the baby. I'm pregnant, and he wasn't very happy about it."

"When's your baby due?"

"In January sometime."

"Why was he mad about the baby?"

"I don't really know. He was angry that I felt sick all the time—and tired. In fact he was furious. I'd never seen him so mad. He started yelling and pushing . . ." Karissa's eyes filled with tears. Holden fought back his own. "He slapped me."

Holden could barely contain his anger. He carefully folded the tea towel and excused himself. He gently closed the back door behind him as he stepped onto the screened-in back porch. He walked to the far wall, and leaning his head against it, he clenched his jaw and closed his eyes against Karissa's pain. He wanted to punch Michael Andrews—a man he didn't even know, a man who lay dead in his grave.

Quickly, Holden stepped outside and walked next door into Karissa's yard. He walked to where he had watched her kneeling by the flower bed that evening he'd first met her. He could see the bud forming out of season on the rosebushes Karissa was so carefully tending. He stooped to take the fragile nub between his fingers. He knew it needed to be pruned, but somehow he couldn't find the courage to do it. Maybe the rosebud was a sign of hope for her. Maybe she was a sign of hope for him.

"Karissa," Holden said softly upon his return to the kitchen, "I want to tell you about my wife."

# Fifteen

"We met," Holden began, "our first year in college. We were taking English comp together. We started dating right away and married at the end of our first year. We were both nineteen—just your age. We were very much in love. I took classes part time that next year and Julie got a job. She worked until she was seven-and-a-half months pregnant with our little boy, Kenneth."

Holden looked up to see Karissa watching him intently from her place opposite him at the kitchen table. She quickly lowered her eyes when he caught her gaze.

"Julie took my truck one afternoon and went for a ride to the mountains, just her and Kenneth. I don't know why. I probably never will. But on her way back down the mountain, the steering went out on the truck. I had warned her many times that the old truck was only for work. It was just an old beater, really. I used it to haul stuff I didn't want to haul in my good truck." Holden took a deep breath.

"She died instantly. Kenneth died a few hours later." Holden looked straight into Karissa's face and waited for her to lift her eyes to meet his. Finally, when she did, he continued. "I thought I'd never live through the pain of the next few months. I didn't want to live through it. I wanted to die. I wanted to be with her and Kenneth, even if it meant death."

Holden paused but only for a moment. "Eventually I learned that if I couldn't get rid of the pain, I could shut it out . . . by feeling nothing."

Karissa's eyes filled with tears as she listened.

"I lived like that for a little over three years. Julie and Kenneth died four years ago. I was twenty-two—almost twenty-three." Holden traced the pattern of the Formica tabletop with his fingers.

"But I met someone who really helped me change. And I met him through a friend. Pastor Jim. Do you know him?"

Karissa nodded.

"Jim and I worked together. He was studying for the ministry and came here to work one summer between school terms. He worked for . . . well, we worked together. He's the one who introduced me to Christ." Holden tried to make his story as clear as possible.

"Let's just say that meeting Christ was the most important thing that ever happened to me in my whole life, including meeting Julie and having Kenneth." Holden sat back and relaxed in his chair. "I can't tell you how important He's become to me. He's helped me deal with my pain, not by shutting it out, but by feeling it completely and knowing that He felt it with me.

"Do you know Jesus, Karissa?" Holden had never shared his faith with anyone before. Somehow, it felt as natural as any conversation he had ever had with anyone. "Do you have anyone who can share your pain?"

Karissa put her head down on her arms and sobs racked her whole body. Holden reached across the table and touched her hair lightly. He found it as soft as it looked. "Do you want to know Christ? Can you let Him help you?"

"I do know Him, Holden. One Sunday in Sunday school I heard my teacher say Jesus died for our sins and if we didn't ask Him into our hearts, we would go to hell when we die. I didn't want to go to hell. I asked Jesus into my heart that day. I want to go to heaven when I die."

"But do you *know* Him, Kassy? Can you say you know Him like you would a friend?"

"No, not like a friend. I think of God, well, as someone up there looking down on all the bad things I've done." Karissa looked up at Holden. "I have always thought of God as mad at me—you know, like my father is."

"He's not like your father. He's not like anyone. He'd like your father to be more like Him, but don't judge God by your dad. That's not fair. And it won't help."

Holden wanted to take Karissa's guilt away.

"But I ran away. I shamed my father."

"We have all shamed our Father; we have all sinned. But you see, that's why Christ came. To help us get rid of the shame. God doesn't want to keep you guilty; He wants to take that guilt. Can you let Him take it, Karissa? Can you give it to Him?"

"Did you feel guilty when Julie died?"

"Oh yes. For two years. I had kept putting off fixing that old truck. She never used it until that day. If I had fixed it like I should have, she would still be alive. At least that's what I thought. But I have no way of knowing that for sure, do I?"

"I feel so guilty for Michael's death. He was so mad at me that night. After we got married he was always mad at me for something. I didn't do anything to suit him. He was miserable and he was sorry he married me."

"Oh? How do you know that?"

"He said so, many times." Karissa blew her nose on a paper towel she found nearby.

"He said that to you?"

"He said lots of things." Karissa dried her eyes and rubbed her forehead. "He said I was a mistake—that I was trying to ruin his life."

"It's not true." Holden found the anger returning. "How can someone as lovely and sensitive as you be a mistake? How could a beautiful young woman like the one sitting right here in front of me ruin anyone's life?" Holden felt embarrassed having said such things to a woman whose husband hadn't even been dead eight weeks yet.

Standing up, Holden moved toward the back door. "I have to go. Tell Aunt Mattie I said good-night, okay? Lock the door behind me."

Karissa followed him to the door. Holden turned and looked down into her clear blue eyes. He found a stray lock of her soft honey blond hair and gently tucked it back into the rest. "Michael Andrews was a fool," he said quietly. "An utter fool."

# Sixteen

"This is going to take longer than I thought," Mark said to Karissa the next day. "The lawyers have filed for a court injunction to freeze all activity on Michael's trust fund and to order an audit. The bank is being cooperative, but it looks like they acted in good faith."

"What does all this mean?" Karissa couldn't understand all that was happening.

"It means that we need to have you stay somewhere Phyllis couldn't possibly find you. As soon as she goes to the bank and finds out that not only are Michael's accounts frozen but so are those I have with her and even the ones she has alone, it could get very rough before it gets better."

"But where would I stay?"

"I've spoken to Pastor Jim and his wife, Linda. They have invited you to stay with them for the weekend, at least. Today's Friday. We have a couple of long days ahead of us before Monday. I wish this had all waited until the beginning of the week, but it can't be helped. She made her move, and we have to be very careful from here on out."

Karissa stood quietly looking out of Mattie and Ben's kitchen window. She knew that a scene with Phyllis would be too stressful on Ben. He was recovering from a slight stroke he had suffered a few months before, and although he was on the mend, it was important that his life be as easy and uncomplicated as possible.

"Everything's going to be all right, honey." Mattie's arms welcomed Karissa. "Don't you worry. You'll see. With Mark and his lawyers handling everything and you staying with Jim and Linda, you couldn't be in better hands."

"Come on now, let's go back over to your place and get some of your things ready. Your mother will have to be told what's happening and that she can reach you at Jim's."

Mark and Mattie went next door with Karissa and helped her get a few things together. Within fifteen minutes she was ready to go.

"I hate to leave my little house," Karissa said as she glanced around the living room on the way out. "It's really become my very own home to me in the last few weeks."

"You'll be back to it soon. I promise." Mark took her arm and guided her through the bright, friendly kitchen, where he and Karissa had enjoyed many conversations together.

———

Jim and Linda Henry were a warm, outgoing couple, much younger than Karissa expected. She barely remembered Jim from their brief introduction, although his words had found a home in her heart. She carried the cherished white card Jim had given her at the funeral in her purse. When she was shown to the small guest room at Jim and Linda's, the first thing she did was get the card out and, after reading it again, slip it under the pillow on the bed that would be hers for the next few nights.

"Think you'll be comfortable here?" Linda's voice had a soft quality about it that Karissa found irresistible.

"Oh yes. This is a charming room. Did you decorate this all yourself?"

"I picked out the paint, and Jim did the painting. I did the trim work and made the curtains. One of the ladies at our church gave me a whole bolt of the fabric. I planned the whole room around that piece of material." Linda laughed. "It's not that easy to make such a strange pattern work, but oh, well. I guess I really liked it when I finally finished."

"It's wonderful." Karissa marveled at the way Linda had decorated around a single piece of fabric, yet the whole room was so perfectly done that the fabric ended up being an accent, not the focus. "What a gift you have!"

"Well, when the budget is as limited as ours, you learn not only to make do, but to make it look like you didn't have to." Karissa liked the way Linda smiled. "The pillows were made from an old gray corduroy coat my grandmother gave me and a red corduroy bedspread my mother was about to throw away. The surface of the bedspread was shot, but the sides were still good. I got a few extra miles out of that old spread and a touch of home in the bargain."

"I like this room . . . very much." It was something her mother would have been able to do, and a style of decorating Phyllis would have found disgusting—unless, that is, a high-priced decorator had suggested it as chic.

The walls were painted a warm shade of gray, the woodwork off-white, almost a cream. The fabric Linda started with was a heavy woven cotton the same cream color as the woodwork with red, black, and gray ovals scattered randomly throughout. Karissa examined the fabric more closely.

"I can't decide," said Linda, "whether they are polka dots, cough drops, or jelly beans!"

"They make this room seem so happy, they must be polka dots or jelly beans!" Karissa said.

"Well, maybe someday we'll know, just by the process of elimination." The two young women laughed and Karissa found it refreshing.

———————

Mark checked into a cheap motel in a small town barely eight miles away. He kept a suitcase packed with the barest essentials for sudden business trips. He left a message with Maria that he wouldn't be home until Tuesday or Wednesday. Alone in his room, he could only imagine what Phyllis was going through with all of their shared bank accounts frozen and Michael's trust fund account closed for audit. If Phyllis had money anywhere else, Mark didn't know of it.

Mark also didn't know that on the afternoon before, Phyllis had seen Mark's car parked at the Hills' home. She had rushed home to get a camera to take a picture of his car, thinking she might be able to use that picture later.

Kate hadn't seen Phyllis outside taking pictures. She was already getting ready for her date with Gerry on Saturday.

For twenty-four hours Kate had been styling and restyling her hair and manicuring her nails. She even soaked her feet and coated them several times, first with Vaseline, then with Jergen's hand lotion. She soaked in a bubble bath on Friday night and again on Saturday afternoon. Jodie was as excited as her mother and helped entertain the smaller children, even taking them next door to watch cartoons so Kate could have an uninterrupted nap in the afternoon.

Kate had the distinct sense that the pieces of her world were coming together nicely.

Phyllis, on the other hand, lived in desperate panic that her whole world was crumbling and falling apart. To make things even worse, Detective Walker was still asking his questions. Disturbing questions.

After all, Michael's death was tragic enough as an accident. But to continue probing and poking around asking all kinds of questions—Phyllis thought it unkind and unnecessary.

Sitting alone in her expensively decorated living room, Phyllis rubbed her finger over the ivory-colored brocade upholstery and down the bleached, carved oak arms of the sofa. What was it Detective Walker had said? She recalled their earlier conversation, word for word.

"Did you ever loan any money to Manny Rodriguez?"

"I loaned money to many of Michael's friends." Phyllis didn't like being questioned by this unfeeling, cold man.

"Did he pay you back?"

"I don't know."

"You don't know?"

"I told him to give the money to Michael."

"Did Michael give you the money back?"

"He probably needed it for something."

"Then, you never got the money back from Manny Rodriguez."

"When you put it like that, no, I guess not."

"Who else did you loan money to?"

"What?"

"You said you often loaned Michael's friends money. Who else did you loan money to?"

"I gave them all money from time to time. It was important to Michael that he not be the only one who had money. He said it wasn't fair to his friends. He was a very giving boy."

"Yes, I know," Walker said sarcastically.

"Pardon me?" Phyllis was on the verge of being insulted.

"Did Manny have reason for being angry with Michael?"

"No, of course not. Michael was as fair and as loyal as they come. All his friends adored him."

"And his wife—did she adore him, too?"

"She chased him all through high school and finally talked him into eloping with her just after she turned nineteen. Of course she adored him; she worshiped the ground he walked on." Phyllis dabbed her eyes with a lace-edged hankie. "We all did."

What did Manny have to do with all this? He wasn't even with the boys when they went swimming. Was he? Did Manny Rodriguez know something about Michael's death that he wasn't telling? Phyllis tried to sort out all the details and the pieces of information she could from the few days following Michael's death when his friends came by. She hardly remembered anything coherently. It had made things so much easier to take the tranquilizers the doctor brought. And, of course, an occasional glass of wine boosted their effect. *Funny, though*, Phyllis mused, *I don't remember Manny coming by at all. In fact, I haven't seen him since.*

# Seventeen

"It's Dad," Jodie said to her mother.

Kate looked at her watch and checked the dial on the clock radio beside the bed. "Right on time. Do I look all right?"

"You look great." Jodie examined Kate's hair and hair-sprayed a small section on the top.

"I'll go on down, then."

"Not yet," Jodie said. "Sammy and Ronnie are laying down the rules. You know, where you'll be, when you'll be home. The usual stuff."

"Oh, my gosh. I'd better get down there." Kate rushed toward her bedroom door.

"Not so fast," Jodie said, standing in her way.

"Jodie," Kate said, "get out of my way."

"In a minute. Let him wait. It won't hurt him. Let's see if he's serious. After all, you can't be too careful these days. It's 1957, for crying out loud. Women have to demand better treatment from their men nowadays."

"Jodie, I'm not kidding. Get out of my way." Kate laughed nervously at her all-too-grown-up fifteen-year-old. There would have been a seventeen-year-old had Kate not miscarried. No matter how many years went by, she still missed the two babies she lost. No one understood her grief, not even Gerry.

"Okay, I guess you can go now." Jodie stepped ceremoniously out of Kate's way.

Gerry stood at the bottom of the stairway waiting

for Kate's entrance. He wasn't disappointed. She looked even more beautiful than he had anticipated.

"Hello, Gerry," Kate said to her husband.

"Good evening, Kathleen." Gerry wanted to take her immediately into his arms, to kiss her and crush her lips with his own. Somehow he managed to be the picture of a perfect and polite suitor. "Are you ready to go?"

"I am."

"And remember, young man," Sammy said with a deep voice to match the solemn expression on his face, "Kathleen is a proper young lady. When you return, before midnight, of course, you must escort her immediately into the house. We don't approve of sitting in the driveway in a parked car any more than sitting anywhere else. She's not home until she's in the house. Is that understood?"

"Yes, sir. Completely." Gerry held out his hand to shake that of his eldest son, who was still a bit shorter than Kate. "With all due respect, sir, I remember the rules."

"See that you do." Sammy looked straight into his father's eyes. "And see that you treat her with respect." Gerry didn't mistake his son's meaning.

"I will, sir. I promise."

Gerry turned to the other children and stretched out his arms for hugs. Lisa was content to stay with Jodie and turned her eyes away from her father when he tried to touch her. Edie wasn't so shy. She flung herself into her father's arms, and he carried her to the door before setting her down next to Ronnie, who just smiled silently at his dad.

"This is quite a family you have here, Kathleen." Gerald Hill looked over the five crowded around the front door. "But isn't there one more somewhere?"

"Yes," Kate said, tears glistening in her eyes, "but she's grown and gone from home."

"You can't be serious. You can't have one older yet than these. You're certainly not old enough to have a grown daughter!"

"Well, thank you, sir, you're too kind."

"I'm learning," Gerry said soberly.

———

After dinner, Gerry suggested they find a place they could talk. Kathleen wasn't willing to go back to the house just yet and knew they couldn't sit in the driveway. She didn't want to give the children any reason to worry. Finally, she suggested Karissa's.

"She's not there, Gerry."

"She's not? Where is she?"

"She's staying with friends for a few days."

"Anything wrong?"

"It's being handled. She's staying with a young pastor and his wife for the weekend. She's in good hands."

"Kate," Gerry said huskily once they were parked next to Karissa's garage. "I've been doing a lot of thinking and I've come to some conclusions about myself." Gerry paused and leaned forward on the steering wheel. Kate waited silently for Gerry to continue.

"I've not been the best husband, I'm afraid. I know that, and I'm sorry."

Kate looked at her hands, held perfectly still in her lap.

"I want to—no, I need to ask your forgiveness. I am so sorry . . . I can't stand . . . I mean . . . I can hardly forgive myself, let alone believe that you could find it in your heart to forgive me . . . but I know unless you do . . . well, I was hoping you'd let me . . ."

"Gerry . . ." Kate hesitated. "I don't know what to say . . . I . . ."

"I'm not asking to come home, Kate. I am only

asking if I could court you for a while. I want to do
this right. I don't deserve this second chance. I know
that. But, Kate, I do love you more than anything.
Please, will you give me the chance to win your hand
again?"

Kate covered her face with her hands and began
to cry softly. Gerry sat motionless, staring first at his
wife, then out the window of the car. "I understand,"
Gerry said at last. "It's too late, isn't it?"

"No, Gerry, it isn't. It's never too late."

"I was afraid that I'd ruined everything between
us . . . I thought . . ."

"You were wrong."

"I know that. I've been wrong for a long time."

"No, I mean you were wrong to think that what we
have between us, the life we have, our family—Gerry,
it's not ruined. It's not too late. But a courtship?
Gerry, are you sure this is what you want?"

"No, it's not what I want. But"—he turned to face
her in the darkness—"it's the least that I can do. It's
what you deserve. Wouldn't you like that, Kate?"

"More than anything. But just knowing you are
willing, that's enough for me."

"Not for me," Gerry said. "I've made you promises
before, and you took me at my word. Not this time.
This time I need to be able to perform on those promises before you take me back. I need to do this—not
only for you but for the kids." Gerry took a deep
breath and then said, "And for me. I need to do this
for me, too."

Kate reached to touch her husband's face, now
wet with tears. He caught her hand and held it to his
face, then moved slightly to press his lips into her
palm. He closed his eyes and held her hand against
his mouth for a long, quiet moment. Finally, he gave
a gentle tug on her hand and she moved easily toward
him. He encircled his precious wife within his arms.

"Kate," Gerry whispered, "Kate." Gerry began covering her face with kisses and she didn't resist. He found her lips with his own and gently pulled her tighter in his arms.

"Gerry," Kate said quietly when he released her from their kiss. "Gerry, are you sure you just want to date? This could be very difficult."

"And very exciting," Gerry said. "We have one thing going for us, Kate. We are married." Gerry pulled her into another long kiss.

"Let's go inside." Kate motioned toward Karissa's house.

"Inside?" Gerry said.

"Let's make some tea. I think we need to be someplace where there's a little more room. I might need to get away from you!" Kate teased.

"Right," Gerry said.

Kate rummaged through her purse until she produced the key to Karissa's house.

Entering Karissa's back door, Kate turned toward Gerry and gently but firmly put her hand on his chest. "Just one thing, Gerry. The bedroom is off limits."

Gerry pushed against her hand and quietly closed the door behind them. "I don't think I heard you."

"Oh yes, you did. And if you don't give me your word, you can take me home this instant."

"Okay, okay." Gerry feigned a pout. "The bedroom's off limits."

Kate turned on the light over the sink and set the teakettle on the burner. She walked to the bathroom and turned on the light, filling the hallway and living room with its soft, indirect glow.

"I've never been in here before," Gerry said as he wandered around. "It's a nice place, isn't it?"

"Karissa loves it."

"I can see why." Gerry looked first into Karissa's

bedroom, then poked his head into the other one. "Sandy staying here too?"

"She's here so Karissa won't be alone at night. She won't be here long; she's leaving for college after the holidays. She's going to Claremont. It's too far to commute, and she doesn't have a car anyway." Kate carried two cups of tea to the living room.

Gerry settled on the comfortable sofa and Kate sat beside him. Gerry sipped his tea in the dimly lit room.

"How's she doing, Kate?" he asked.

"She's going through a bad time, Gerry. She's a lot stronger than I thought she'd be. But then . . ."

"Go on," Gerry said.

Kate closed her eyes and sat very still. Then she shook her head and looked into Gerry's eyes.

"What is it, Kate?" Gerry asked gently. "Is there something you're not telling me?"

"Are you sure you want to hear all this tonight?"

"All what?"

"All about Karissa. I know how you feel about . . ."

"I've been so wrong. Help me make it right, okay?"

"If you're sure."

"I have to start somewhere. Let me start with Karissa." Gerry took Kate's face in his hands. "First, though, let me tell you how much I love you, Kathleen."

Kate moved easily into his embrace and let his kiss linger. Pulling a little way back, she took a deep breath. "Maybe I should sit on the other side of the room."

"Don't, Kate. I want you close. Is that okay?"

"Of course." Kate relaxed against her husband's shoulder. He put his arm around her, and turning, she snuggled her back tight against his chest.

"Okay, now tell me everything."

Kate gave a deep sigh. "Michael wasn't good to

Karissa, Gerry," she began. She told him of the bruises she found on Kassy's back, thigh, and face. She told him about the twisted ankle and the marks left on Kassy's arms by Michael's strong hands. As she continued, Gerry couldn't hold back his tears. "And . . ."

"And? You mean there's more?"

"Karissa's going to have a baby, Gerry. Michael's baby."

"I knew it."

"No, Gerry, you didn't. She's only six months along. I took her to the doctor myself. She couldn't have been pregnant when they married. From the things she told me it's pretty obvious she was . . . well, inexperienced when they eloped."

"You sure?"

"Positive." Kate pulled away from Gerry's embrace. She took a moment, then stood up. Slowly, she walked across the living room and sat in the easy chair facing him. He could barely make out her features in the dim light. "Gerry," she said softly.

"Yes?"

"We did this to her as much as Michael did."

"You think so?"

"Yes. I do. I didn't know what to tell her. I suspected he was hitting her. I mean, the few times I saw her this summer, I could tell."

"How did you know?"

"I heard my own words coming out of her mouth."

"I don't understand."

"Gerry, this is hard for me to say. It's going to be hard for you to hear."

"I'm listening."

"I heard Karissa give the same excuses I had used when you . . ."

"Oh, my God. My God." Gerry leaned forward. Putting his elbows on his knees, he buried his face in his hands, sobs of remorse and guilt wracking his body. "I'm sorry, Kate. I'm so sorry. God, please . . . forgive me."

"And, me, too, dear God," Kate said, her voice breaking.

Gerry looked up at his wife. "You? Kate, you have nothing . . . you've done nothing wrong. It's all my fault. Don't you feel guilty, Kate. Please, don't you feel guilty, too."

"But I am, Gerry. It's as much my fault as yours."

"That's not true!"

"If I had stopped you sooner. If I hadn't excused it . . . if I hadn't . . ." Kate stopped. "But I didn't know. Gerry, my own father did what he called 'keeping the family in line,' just like you do."

"Did," Gerry said flatly. "What I *did*."

"I tried to tell my mother, and she told me I had to learn your moods. That it was my responsibility to find out what set you off and to make sure that I never crossed that line. That's how she managed my father. Or so she said. But we lived terrified of him, Gerry. Just as I've been terrified of you. And," she continued, "just as Karissa was terrified of Michael."

Gerry quickly crossed the room and knelt in front of his wife. "Kate, I truly repent. Is it too late? Have I lost the love and respect of my family forever?"

"It's never too late, Gerry. We've looked at the Bible as a rule book all our lives. We've tried to live by the discipline, to follow the commandments to the letter. We accepted God's Word as something we had to measure up to . . . and we were right, up to a point."

"We missed something, didn't we, Kate? At least I did."

"Do you know what it is?"

"Grace. Mercy. Unconditional love. Security. Joy. Peace."

"What?"

"I have been reading the Bible from the front to the back. I've never done that before in my entire life." Sitting at her feet, Gerry laid his head in Kate's lap. "I can't believe I tried to live a godly life, when I hadn't even read the instruction book."

Kate laughed.

"What's so funny?"

"It's just like the time you tried to put the swing set together without reading the instructions. Remember how frustrating that was?"

"That's the way I lived my entire life. Except my work—if I hadn't read the instructions there, I would have been electrocuted by now."

"Gerry, don't you think we could put our marriage back together if we read the book?"

"It's not a marriage I want with you, Kate."

"It's not?" Kate looked confused.

"No, it's not. It's a relationship. A deep, intimate relationship. I've been thinking about what a wonderful woman you are. How gifted you are with the children and how well you manage the household. If I were to rate you, as a man rates his employees, I'd say you maintain a high standard of quality performance at your job." Gerry looked up into Kate's face. "What I am saying, Kathleen, is this—I have a high respect for you as a person."

"You do?"

"That surprises you, doesn't it?"

"It . . . I mean, well, yes, it does."

"I didn't even realize it myself. As you so clearly pointed out to me, I was so busy trying to maintain my position as head of the house, I almost forgot that you are the heartbeat of the home."

"I didn't realize . . . ." Kate stopped, unable to go on.

"That's just the problem, I didn't either. I suffered

a blow to the head, you know, when you spoke to me that night. But later, after I had prayed and read the verses you underlined in my Bible, I realized that I had stabbed my home—my marriage—right in the heart. Not just once, but time and time again. I saw that when a man loves his wife, he loves himself. That as a man lays down his life for his wife, she gives life back to him."

"My whole life is you, Gerry."

"I know that, Kate. And it's a miracle. An absolute miracle." Gerry stood and pulled Kate to her feet. Gently taking her in his arms, he slowly lowered his lips to cover hers. As he gently kissed her, they pressed their bodies tightly together and let their tears mingle freely.

"What's going on here?" The deep voice boomed as the bright overhead light blazed on.

Gerry and Kate jumped apart and faced the strange man poised in the doorway with a heavy crescent wrench gripped in his hand.

"Who are you?" Gerry said.

"That's what I was about to ask you." Holden stepped into the room. "Mr. Hill?"

"Yes, and this is my wife, Kate." Gerry squinted against the brightness of the light. "Who are you . . . Holden Kelley?"

"I saw the lights on over here. Karissa isn't home. I didn't . . . what are you doing here?"

"Karissa . . . I'm Karissa's mother," Kate said.

"I'm confused," Gerry said.

"I am too," Holden responded.

"Let's get this straight. How did you get in Karissa's house?" Gerry asked. "Do you know my daughter?"

"My aunt lives next door. She and Mark Andrews asked me to take care of Karissa's yard."

"You?" Gerry nodded toward Holden. "You're one

of the best landscape architects in the county. I can hardly see you mowing people's lawns for a living."

"He didn't mean for me to do it. He knows I have a residential crew or two. But I do my aunt's yard myself and when I met Karissa, I thought it best to . . . to . . . well, I decided to do it myself."

"I see. What are you doing here this time of night?"

"I guess you've not told him everything, then?" Holden directed his question to Kate.

"There's more?" Gerry asked.

"I think I'd better reheat the water. This could take a while," Kate said as she went back into the kitchen.

"It's Mrs. Andrews," Holden began. "She's a real piece of work, let me tell you." Holden took a sip of the hot tea Kate offered, settled back in his chair, and began to fill Karissa's parents in on most of the latest information.

# Eighteen

Kate stretched leisurely in her bed. She had been awake most of the night reliving her "date" with Gerry. She looked forward to having him come for Sunday dinner. Although the family usually attended church on Sunday morning, she had decided that on this special occasion they would all stay home.

Jodie was already fixing some Jell-O and baking a chocolate cake. Kate could smell the cake all the way upstairs. The kids seemed to be as excited to see their father as Kate was. Her house hadn't seemed this happy in a long time.

Sammy slammed the back door as he came in. Jodie had given him and Ronnie a five-dollar bill and instructions to ride their bikes to the bakery less than a mile away for donuts. Soon Kate could smell coffee perking and wished she hadn't agreed to stay in bed until the children called her. Lisa was shrieking and Edie poked her head in for permission to climb in bed with Kate.

She could hear the small brigade making its way up the stairs, and she and Edie pretended to be asleep. Once the door opened, and four of Kate's six children tiptoed to the foot of her bed, Kate opened her eyes to their smiling faces as they stood holding a breakfast tray.

"That's for Mom!" Jodie scolded Edie and grabbed her arm. "Yours is downstairs."

"I want a chocolate one," Edie demanded.

"It's right downstairs, on the table, waiting for you. Unless Ronnie gets there first," Jodie said.

"No! It's mine!" Edie screamed as she bounced toward the edge of Kate's bed.

"Careful, you'll spill the coffee!" Jodie demanded.

Kate laughed as Ronnie and four-year-old Edie raced through the bedroom door and disappeared.

"I'd better make sure they don't kill each other," Sammy said as he followed close behind them.

"He's so grown-up," Kate mused.

"Don't kid yourself, Mom. He wants another donut." Kate watched Jodie toss her hair behind her shoulder with a graceful movement of her head. Lisa, the baby, clung to her sister as she sat quietly beside her mother.

"You really had a good time, Mom?"

"Yes, honey. I really had a good time."

"Is he coming home?"

"I hope so."

"Hope? Don't you know for sure?"

"He wants to wait awhile. Just to be sure."

"Wait for what?" Jodie played with Lisa's soft blond curls, tucking them behind the baby's ear.

"I'll let him tell you himself." Kate wasn't sure she could manage a satisfactory explanation herself. It was more something she felt than thought. How could she explain feelings?

"Is that okay with you?"

"Is what okay with me? That he come home, or that he wait awhile?"

"Both."

"Yes." Kate watched her daughter's face. "On both counts."

"I don't understand."

"I'm not sure I do either, sweetheart. But it feels good. It's almost like having a boyfriend again. You know what I mean?"

"Not really." Jodie looked away from her mother and smiled slightly. Lisa shifted on her sister's lap, her eyes closed and her thumb stuck firmly in her mouth.

"I bet." Kate grinned at her fifteen-year-old, who seemed to get prettier every day. Jodie's dark, straight hair was a lot like Gerry's, full and coarse. Jodie had given up her thick braids for a softer, almost bobbed style. She rolled the ends under on heavy metal curlers and kept her bangs cut straight across her forehead. Dark eyebrows arched naturally above her long black lashes. Her hazel eyes often made her appear brooding, almost mysterious. Judging by appearances, few people would think she and Karissa, with her fine blond hair and bright blue eyes, were related, but their gentle temperaments gave away the fact that they were sisters. Kate knew Jodie was already catching many glances from the boys at school.

"Mom?"

"Yes?"

"Am I too young to have a boyfriend?"

"A little, yes. Do you?"

"Do I what?"

"Have a boyfriend?"

"Well, sort of." Jodie shifted and pulled sleeping Lisa closer.

"I see."

"We're not going steady or anything."

"That's good." Kate sipped her coffee.

"But he does walk me to class once or twice a day."

"Hmmm."

"And, he wants me to meet him after school for a Coke sometimes."

"I see."

"Do you think that'd be all right?"

"I don't know. What do you think?"

"There's nothing wrong with it, is there? I mean, all we do is . . . I mean, all we *would* do is go to the fountain at Gray's drugstore and have a Coke."

"Alone?"

"Hardly! Everybody goes there."

"Can I think about it?"

"Sure." Jodie walked toward the bedroom door, holding Lisa. "Could you think about it before Friday?"

"I'll tell you Wednesday, okay?"

"Morning?"

Kate laughed. "Wednesday morning. I promise."

Jodie gave Kate a broad smile and then impulsively threw her a kiss. "Thanks, Mom."

"And, Jodie? Thank you," Kate said, "for breakfast."

"Can I get the roast on? We learned how last year in Miss Smith's home ec. class."

"Gladly. Help yourself." Kate snuggled deeper into her pillows. She heard Jodie put Lisa in her crib and then go downstairs. Turning on her side, she felt suddenly content. She stretched her arm toward the empty side of the bed. Gerry's side. She looked forward to having him be with them for the day. But she looked forward even more to having him come home to stay.

Just before she dozed off, Kate decided to see Dr. Milford. She wanted Gerry, but she had had plenty of his babies. Certainly Dr. Milford would understand.

---

Mark Andrews had asked Gerry to meet with him and Holden for an early breakfast, and Gerry had reluctantly agreed. At the diner the men awkwardly shook hands, and Holden told Mark he had not filled Gerry in on all the particulars about Karissa's financial affairs. He didn't quite understand it all himself and offered to excuse himself while the two men discussed the situation.

"I wouldn't hear of such a thing," Mark said emphatically. "You're a smart businessman. I'd like to hear what you have to say about this."

Mark Andrews had hired both these exceptional men to do subcontracting work on his construction projects. He had the highest regard for their work. But on a personal level, Mark struggled with his feelings toward Gerry. Knowing some of Gerry's treatment of his wife and family, he couldn't help but be angry. He even found himself jealous of the man, mostly because of Kate. But his good sense told him if he wanted to overcome his inner struggle about Kate, it would be a smart move to be as good a friend as possible to her husband.

"It's a mess, all right," Holden said. "You might take a loss on this. How serious is it?"

"Pretty serious. I'm afraid I've turned much too much control over to my wife." Mark noticed a slight frown crease Gerry's forehead.

"And I haven't given mine enough . . ." Gerry said absentmindedly.

"Excuse me?" Mark said.

"Nothing, just a thought. I guess I'm still unsure how all this affects Karissa."

"In the long run, it won't affect her as much as it does right now. I'm afraid all my personal assets are tied up, and could be for quite some time. It depends on how much trouble Phyllis and her lawyers give me."

"That means that Kassy is without any way to support herself?"

"And I'm almost helpless to help her," Mark said.

"What about her personal checking, or perhaps a savings account. Did Michael. . . ?"

Holden sat quietly while Mark answered Gerry's questions.

"Michael spent as much as his mother gave him. And it looks like that was plenty. What's worse—*she* spent what Michael didn't." Gerry shook his head as Mark continued. "What a fool I've been. I have made so many mistakes."

"Who hasn't?" Gerry said. "I know I have. Perhaps if we had taken more of an interest . . . if I hadn't been so stubborn . . ."

"Let's not get into a blaming game, Mr. Hill," Holden said. "From what I can see, there's been quite enough guilt all around. Self-blame won't get you anywhere."

"He's right, Gerry. God only knows how much of this is my fault. But looking back won't get either of us anywhere. It's Kassy we have to be concerned about now. Kassy and the baby."

"The baby." Gerry had almost forgotten about the baby. "I wonder if she'll even let me near the baby."

"Pardon?" Holden said.

"I have made so many mistakes. Raising my family, I mean. I don't know if there is any hope for—"

"There's always hope, Mr. Hill," Holden said. "Always." Holden checked his watch. "I need to be going. I'll be late for church." Holden took out his wallet and glanced at Gerry, who was about to protest. "This is on me today, Mr. Hill. I won't hear another word." Holden grabbed the check. "See you at church?"

"You probably will," said Mark. "But I might be a few minutes late. Save me a place?"

Holden laughed. "Glad to. But I hardly think it's necessary." The school auditorium was more than adequate for the seventy-five or so worshipers that met there each Sunday.

"I don't know. The place seems more crowded each Sunday."

"I didn't know you were a churchgoer, Andrews," Gerry said.

"Well, sir. There's a lot you don't know about me."

"I know you're an honest man. Run a tight business. And I know you to be more than fair with your subcontractors."

"You know, Gerry, I always thought of myself as a Christian. I don't cheat anyone, I don't pad my tax returns, and I don't chase women."

Gerry took a swallow of lukewarm coffee. "Yeah, I know what you mean."

"I've provided more than enough for my family to live on. Thanks mostly to having a good start by selling some of my dad's land."

Gerry listened as Mark continued. "But I found out the hard way, that's not enough." Mark played with his fork. "I paid too much attention to my business, and not enough to my family. Phyllis was so difficult, I gave in to her. I let her lead me around by the nose. Oh, not so that anyone could tell. But she really called the shots at home. I didn't just work to make more money—I worked long and hard so I wouldn't have to deal with her. The more money I made, the more she spent. I kept busy making it to keep her busy spending it. It seemed to work out. I didn't bother her, she didn't bother me." Mark paused and Gerry noticed the tears threatening to spill from his eyes. "And look at the price I—we—paid for our selfishness. We lost our son."

Mark pulled out a large handkerchief and blew his nose. "I can't ever get back those years. I just hope I don't lose touch with my grandchild. I can't tell you how much Karissa's baby means to me. It's really a bright spot of hope in a very dark and hopeless situation."

"I don't know how I feel about it." Gerry was as honest as he could be. "Here she is, my oldest daughter. She's going to be a mother and I can't even help her out. I barely make enough to keep the family at home going. Much less take on another baby. Our youngest is only two, or nearly two. I'm losing track." Gerry laughed. "We have six, you know. Five still at home."

"I know. It's amazing. Kate still looks . . ." Mark let his comment die unfinished.

"She's a wonderful woman. I have so much to be thankful for. I almost lost it all, Mark. I almost lost it all . . ." Mark waited silently for Gerry to continue.

"I did just the opposite of what you did. Oh, I worked hard."

"No one knows that better than me, Gerry. You're the best electrical contractor I've ever worked with."

"Thanks. But at home, I ran my family much like I ran my men. I was the boss, all right. Totally. And I enforced that position far too often. I treated Kate like I had to keep her in line. Like she was some stubborn, willful woman. That if I didn't take a firm hand with her, she'd—"

The waitress came by with fresh coffee and Mark held up his cup for a refill. When she walked away, Gerry finished his thought. "I was so wrong. I have asked her to give me another chance."

"Are you moving back in?"

"Not just yet. I think I need to give her some time—and the kids too."

"Time for what?"

"To show—not just promise them—that I'm changing. Time for me too. Time for me to stand back and appreciate them. I might even ask her to marry me again."

"Marry? You're not divor—"

"No. Nothing like that. It's the idea of it. A new beginning. I didn't do such a hot job with my vows the first time. I want to say them again, and this time in front of the kids. I realized these past several weeks that I wasn't only mistreating Kate, but my whole family. Karissa's the worst of it, though. It may be too late. She probably wouldn't give me the time of day, let alone another chance."

"Don't be too sure." Mark checked his watch. "Hey, how about goin' to church with us? It's nothing fancy, I must warn you. But I tell you, that young pastor really has a good head on his shoulders. You may know him—Jim Henry—he works for me on occasion. The church called him here but can't afford to pay him a living wage. He works now and again to make ends meet."

"No kidding."

"And I think of how much money I've sunk into projects at the church Phyllis and I attend—or used to. I have given a lot of money for a brass chandelier, an average working man's month's pay to put in a new velvet drape, and a large chunk of change for a hand-carved table just to put flowers on." Mark shook his head. "I guess I don't regret having been generous with God's house, but it doesn't seem right somehow. I mean, can God be pleased with decorating one of his houses so well, when across town they don't even have a building of their own?"

Gerry grinned. Mark was more down-to-earth than he had ever thought. Perhaps Gerry Hill wasn't the only one who was changing.

"How about it, Hill. Join me for church?"

"Maybe some other time, okay?" Gerry could barely stand sleeping without Kate; going to church without her was out of the question.

"Hey, I'll hold you to that." Mark grinned and left a generous tip on the table for the waitress. "Any longer here and we'd be paying rent," he laughed as he turned to leave Gerry alone.

*Karissa, what have I done to you? How can I make it up to you?* Gerry stared into his cold coffee and refused the waitress's offer of a warm up. *I guess I'll tackle one thing at a time. Kate comes first.*

# Nineteen

"Excuse me, Mr. Kelley?"

Holden turned to face the approaching man. "Yes, I'm Holden Kelley."

"May I have a word with you?"

Holden glanced toward the school gymnasium. "I'm on my way to church."

"I'll only take a minute of your time, Mr. Kelley. I'm Hal Walker." Walker flashed his badge toward Holden. "I'm investigating the death of Michael Andrews."

"I see. How can I help you?" Holden gave Walker his full attention.

"I understand you might know Manny Rodriguez."

"He's worked for me from time to time. He's still in college, so I haven't been able to use him full time."

"What do you know about Manny?"

"Not much. Good worker. Kind of quiet. Responsible, I'd say. He's mentioned coming from a large family, lots of brothers, sisters, cousins. I guess that's about all I can tell you."

"He was a friend of Michael Andrews. Did you know that?"

"No, I didn't. But then I probably wouldn't. I don't get much into the personal lives of my men."

"Would you say Manny has a temper?"

"Not that I've ever noticed. He's a quiet sort. Smiles easily. I haven't heard him enter into conversations much. He seems an attentive listener, though."

"He ever have a girl?"

"Couldn't say."

"You never saw him with a girl, then?"

"I only saw him at work. Except for the time I ran into him at the county fair with his sister and her kids. Seems like a pretty normal kid to me." Holden paused. "Why all these questions about Manny? How is he connected to the Andrews accident?"

"Not sure," Walker said. "It's just that he came by and spoke to the young Mrs. Andrews the night her husband died. The other boys don't recall seeing him after that, although Mrs. Andrews said he left her place to find them."

"That's interesting."

"What's more, she said he was angry at Michael."

"Angry? Why?"

"Can't say for sure. But he came after the beating. Suppose he could have been angry about that?"

"What beating?"

"Didn't you know? Michael worked that pretty young wife of his over pretty good the night he died. The officers on the case said she had a black eye and quite a swollen ankle. Even thought it might be broken. She had bruises on both her arms."

Holden suddenly felt ill as anger welled up in him, anger at Michael for all the pain he had caused Karissa.

Walker checked his note pad, then lifted his head and looked steadily at Holden, as if studying his reaction to this information. "You ever know Andrews to beat his wife before this?"

"I didn't know them—I only met Mrs. Andrews after her husband's death."

"That so?"

"In fact I've only known her a couple of weeks. I

knew she had trouble with a swollen ankle, but I thought it might be because of the baby."

"She's pregnant?"

"Yeah."

"He beat his pregnant wife?"

Holden clenched his jaw against the pain of what Karissa had endured. "Great guy, wouldn't you say?"

"Have you seen Manny Rodriguez since Andrews' death?"

"Nope. I heard he left town. I called him about a job, and his mother said he was looking for work in L.A."

"Left town?"

"That's what she said." Holden looked around to see Mark's car pull into the parking lot. "Have you talked to Mark Andrews about this?"

"Not yet. Still checking around first. I'll get to him later." Walker put his note pad in his jacket pocket. "Listen, if you hear from Manny, I'd appreciate a call. I have a few questions for him." Walker held out his card.

"Sure thing."

"And, if you think of anything else . . ."

"I'll let you know."

"Thanks." As he walked to his car, Walker nodded toward Mark Andrews.

"What's that all about?" Mark said as he reached Holden's side.

"Did you know they're investigating Michael's death?"

"Haven't given it much thought." Mark looked at the unmarked car driving away. "I guess they'd have to, wouldn't they? It was a strange accident. Guess they have to cover all the bases. What'd he want with you?"

"He was asking about Manny Rodriguez."

"You know, I haven't seen Manny. He didn't come to the funeral, and he hasn't been by. The other boys have all stopped by to see us. They've asked about Karissa. They haven't bothered her that I know of." Mark and Holden walked toward the gym doors. Piano music could be heard coming from within. "They have all been quite sobered by what happened to Michael. They were a pretty wild bunch in high school. Football players the lot of them."

"Mark, did you know Karissa was . . . well, that . . . I don't know how to ask you this."

"Shoot straight, Holden. What do you want to know?"

"Did you know Michael hit Karissa the night he died?"

"He didn't hit her, Holden. He beat her up. I saw her the next day. If he hadn't already been dead, I might have killed him myself. I was so angry. Somehow that anger helped get me through the next few days. Strange, isn't it? Instead of being ashamed of him, I was mad. Later, I felt the shame of it all. Keeping busy trying to help Karissa get her affairs in order has helped me, even though it hasn't helped her all that much."

Mark paused before opening the gym door. "There's got to be an answer in all this mess."

"Well, one thing for sure," Holden said. "We're in the right place to listen."

Mark gave Holden a warm smile and a pat on the back as they entered the River Place Community Church together.

───────

"Good word, Jim." Holden pumped the hand of the young minister after the service.

"Sure was," Mark agreed. "Faith isn't something I've had a lot of these past few weeks. You gave me a new way to look at it. Thanks."

"How's Karissa?" Holden asked.

"She's just not ready to come yet," Jim said, motioning to Linda. "I was just telling these two concerned men that Karissa stayed home this morning."

"She's not ready to come to church just yet," Linda agreed. "Let's give her a little more time. I think she's got lots of questions that need answering first. We've spent a lot of time just talking."

"She really needs a friend right now."

"She certainly does . . ." Sandy said, joining the group. "She needs someone who can answer her questions a lot better than I can."

"We're going to ask her to stay with us for a week or so," Linda went on. "She's working through a lot of pain and we want to be there for her."

"I think that's great," said Mark. "It'll give me time to take care of the details and work out the problems with Phyllis. I feel a lot better knowing Phyllis doesn't know where Karissa is."

"That bad, huh?" Jim asked.

"Worse, I'm afraid. My lawyers are working all weekend with an auditor. They're trying to figure out what in the world she's done and assess how bad the damage is. Not only to Michael's money, but to mine. Money does bad things to people."

"It's not the money, Mark," Jim said, "it's the motives. The intent of the heart can be much more destructive than we realize. What about your parents—didn't they have money? Weren't they good people?"

"The best. Money never was an issue. They lived well, but not . . . I guess you would say *above* like Phyllis does. She has this need. No, drive. She is driven to live above everyone."

"She has paid a pretty high price, wouldn't you say?" Holden asked.

"She doesn't even know how high yet. None of us will until the auditors give us a report."

"And when will that be?"

"I'll talk to my accountant tonight, he'll tell me how much work there is left to do. We have a meeting with the lawyers tomorrow morning."

"And how are you doing, Mark?" Jim sounded concerned.

"I'm *doing.* That's all, Pastor. Just doing."

"How is it at home?" Jim asked Mark.

"I'm not at home. I'm staying at a motel on the edge of town for a while. I need some time alone. I've been doing a lot of thinking—and praying."

"Let me know if you need anything, okay?"

"Thanks, Jim. I probably will have some questions later. And I want to see Karissa. Could I come by later?"

"She'd like that."

"How about supper?" Linda offered.

"I don't want you to go out of your way . . ."

"Nonsense. I'll expect you around six-thirty. I'll tell Karissa; it'll brighten her day." Linda turned to Holden. "How about you? Want to join us?"

"Thanks, but I'm leaving town for a few days."

"How's that?" Mark asked.

"I've a job to check on in L.A. It'll take several weeks."

"I knew you'd outgrow us here," Mark teased. "They've heard about your work in the city. Small-town boy makes good in the big city."

Holden smiled and let Mark, Jim, and Linda assume whatever they wished. Karissa needed time, and he could give her that time while taking care of the job in L.A. In his off hours, he could try to track down Manny. He might run from the police, but Holden was pretty sure Manny wouldn't run from him.

# Twenty

The news from the accountant wasn't good. Mark was trying to make decisions that would protect his assets from further erosion due to Phyllis's excessive spending habits. His stockbroker had no idea Mark didn't even know about the stocks Phyllis had sold. There had really been no need to notify him since only one signature was required at the brokerage house. Phyllis had insisted on that arrangement once when Mark needed to make an emergency capital investment in some land and equipment and stocks needed to be liquidated. "It just makes things more efficient on such short notice," she had explained.

Phyllis had managed to almost wipe out Mark's personal funds and had borrowed so heavily against Michael's trust that bankruptcy seemed unavoidable.

Mark's lawyers insisted he move back home, so in case Phyllis tried to sue for divorce, she couldn't claim Mark abandoned her, or try to make excessive claim to the house.

"Lay low for a while until we figure out what to do," they said. "Pacify her if you can. Tell her anything to keep her from asking too many questions. At the same time, see if you can get her to tell you anything. Meanwhile, convert all the assets you can into nonliquid investments. Take only a living allowance instead of a full salary for a while. Tell her you've tied up your assets as security on another project. Anything to keep her happy. Tell her you stand to make a great deal of money—anything! Buy us some time!"

Mark knew he wouldn't lie to Phyllis. Her deceit had already caused him overwhelming financial challenges; he wasn't about to make it worse by stooping to her level.

"We're having a momentary financial cash flow problem," he told her a few nights later. "I'm sure it's nothing to worry about. But for now, I'll only be giving you just enough to keep the household running. You'll need to cut Maria to a couple of days each week for a while."

"I can't do that!" Phyllis's eyes sparked with anger.

"You have no choice, my dear." Mark tried to keep his voice even. "I told you, it won't be for long. Just until this . . . well, this situation blows over."

"Did you make another blunder, Mark? I can't believe how such a talented contractor can be so financially inept. What's the problem? Haven't I solved them for you before?"

Mark fought to keep his anger under control. "Thanks anyway. But you see, there's some problem with Michael's estate. . . ."

Phyllis spun around to face him, her wine glass nearly empty. "A problem?" Her face was pale and Mark thought he detected a twitch tug at the corner of her mouth.

"Not a big one, I'm sure. It's just a little snag, that's all. Something about Michael never signing over the beneficiary to Karissa. As you say, I've never been much good at financial things. Somehow the bank has assumed *they* were named as beneficiary. Do you know how that could have happened?"

"It was just a technicality, Mark."

"A technicality?"

"You see, when we borrowed the money for

Michael's car, we secured it with the trust fund."

"I didn't know we borrowed money for Michael's car."

"You thought I paid cash for a Crown Victoria?"

"I watched you write out the check. The dealer thought we paid cash. I remember how you made such a big deal of . . ." Mark let his last comment die.

"I did write out a check—on money secured with Michael's trust. I'm sure we discussed it, Mark. I discussed all our financial affairs with you. Surely you remember . . . but then, you were so often preoccupied with your work. I may not have pressed you with the details." Phyllis poured her glass full again.

"I guess not." Mark eyed his wife with new suspicion. "What did you do with the rest of the money? Surely the amount borrowed against the trust covered more than just his car. That was over two years ago. Only the interest payments have been made. The outstanding principal is almost equal to the fund. Do you know how that happened?"

"Well, of course I do. Michael needed money for the down payment on the house. I told you that." Mark's inquiries were obviously making Phyllis nervous.

"No, you didn't. You told me, and everyone else in town, that *we* gave Michael and Karissa the money."

"Come on, Mark. You didn't believe that we had that kind of money, did you?"

"No, I didn't. But then, you were handling the family finances. You said we did. I let it go at that." Mark watched his wife nervously twirl the remaining drink in her long-stemmed cocktail glass.

"And the remodeling?"

"I had to hire that done, Mark. You're far too busy with your housing developments to bother with that yourself. I used a smaller contractor, one who specializes in remodeling."

"And the decorator?"

"I got a very good deal there, Mark. You know he did this house at the same time—he almost threw in the cost of Michael's house as a favor to me."

"I bet."

"What do you mean by that?"

"I can't see the most expensive decorator in town throwing in anything for free. And this house—did you decorate our house with Michael's money?"

"Of course not. His money was never touched. The principal is safe and sound in the bank."

"Not anymore it's not."

"What?"

"Remember, the beneficiary was changed. The bank is foreclosing on the trust fund, Phyllis. Because of your excessive compulsions and your insatiable appetite for the very best of everything, the bank is *inheriting* Michael's money. Money that should have gone to Karissa."

"That girl!" Phyllis swallowed the remaining alcohol in her glass and poured it full once more. "She's been out to get our money from the start."

"*Our* money?" Mark could hardly believe she'd even use the term. "Well, that's not a worry anymore, Phyllis."

"It's not?"

"There's no money for her to get. You already got it all."

"She'll be all right, Mark. She's got the house, hasn't she? That's paid for. Let her sell the house. She'll have more money than she's ever dreamed of having. That'll last until she can find another hus—"

"No!" Mark was almost unable to control himself. Taking a deep breath, he continued in a soft tone, "It's her home now. We'll sell the car. That'll keep her going for a while."

"That's exactly what I thought. I asked her to sign

over the title so we could do that if we needed to. I'm not sure she ever gave it back to me. I'll go over first thing in the morning and take care of it." Phyllis smiled sweetly at her husband.

"I already did," Mark said flatly.

"Pardon me?"

"I already took care of it." Mark wasn't about to tell Phyllis he had arranged not only for the sale of the car but also for the purchase of another, smaller car for Karissa.

"Oh," Phyllis said quietly. "What do you plan to do about the finances with the business?"

"Malcolm is checking into it now," Mark said. Malcolm had tried to warn him about Phyllis's spending habits on several occasions. Being the Andrewses' accountant wasn't the most pleasant job, especially when Mark had refused to pay attention to what his wife had been doing for years.

"Oh?" Phyllis acted nonchalant, but there was no concealing the fear in her eyes.

"He's seeing what stocks we can liquidate. Don't worry. We'll manage. It'll take a few weeks, that's all." Mark watched for Phyllis's reaction. She remained composed.

"Why didn't you come to me sooner?" Phyllis asked.

"I didn't know sooner. I found out right after Michael's death. I didn't want to bother you. You were having a hard enough time as it was."

"It's really not a good time to sell our stocks, Mark. Isn't there another way? I mean, what about a business loan?"

"I've never borrowed money, Phyllis."

"I know."

"My father left me enough money to build a good business and make a decent living without speculating on the bank's money or gambling with the future.

The construction business is risky enough without—"

"Others do it all the time! It's the way you—"

"I'm not others, Phyllis. It was not my father's way, and it's not my way." Mark picked up the newspaper and turned to the want ad section. "Malcolm will give me the advice I need. After what you've done with Michael's trust fund, I don't think I want to hear financial advice from you right now."

Mark watched Phyllis set her glass on the bar and trace the rim with her finger. She turned to leave the room and Mark stopped her.

"You'd better pick that glass up yourself. I already cut Maria's schedule."

Phyllis slowly turned and faced Mark. She watched him calmly read his paper, then spun suddenly around, picked up her wine glass, and threw it directly into the mirror above the bar. The glass exploded, sending imported lead crystal slivers in every direction and leaving a spider web pattern in the expensive beveled mirror.

Mark didn't even lower his paper. Phyllis turned and calmly walked from the room. Mark heard the bedroom door close softly, and the definite click as she, unnecessarily, locked him out of their bedroom.

Mark knew from experience it would be a house of silence for days, perhaps even weeks to come. It had wounded him in the past—he welcomed it now.

# Twenty-one

In the following weeks, Karissa welcomed the tender companionship of Linda Henry. A solid friendship emerged and the two young women talked excitedly about the coming of Karissa's baby and the hope that one day soon Linda and Jim would also be expecting their first child. Karissa often wondered and listened for news about Holden's absence but didn't think it appropriate to ask about it.

Mark surprised Karissa with a small 1955 Thunderbird and coaxed her out to practice driving. Mark was a gentle and patient coach, and Karissa soon found the courage to drive on those occasions when Linda needed something from the market.

Finally, just before Thanksgiving, Karissa decided to go back to her own house. The money Mark deposited in her account after selling Michael's car, along with what he had given her just after the funeral, was enough to manage for a while. She knew decisions had to be made soon, and if she had to sell the house, she wanted to make the decision while living there.

Mark seldom spoke of Phyllis, although Karissa knew they were still together. In some ways, Karissa wanted them to work out their differences. After all, even though her own parents were still "courting," they were happier than they had been in years. Or so Kate said. Karissa had yet to face her father. She could still hear the hurtful things he had said to her when he found out she had married Michael. No matter what happened between her parents, she knew she could never go home again.

"I want you to come home for Thanksgiving, Kassy," Kate said one afternoon over tea. Karissa was glad to be home in her own little house, sharing the lovely afternoon with her mother.

"I don't know, Mama. I don't know if I want to see—"

"You need to see him, Karissa. He's changed."

"You say that, but . . ."

"I mean it, Kassy. He's changed."

"I just don't see how it will make any difference. I mean, now that I have my own home, and my own baby on the way . . . I just don't want to . . ."

"It will make a difference because he is different. We've been 'dating' for over a month now. I have never been treated this way before. He's considerate. He's a perfect gentleman. He's even attending church with me up at River Place Community and he's seeing Pastor Jim weekly for an early breakfast."

"You're going to River Place? Linda didn't tell me."

"We were hoping you'd come too. We asked her not to tell you—we thought you might stay away if you thought you'd run into your father."

"I would."

"Kassy, please, honey. Pray about it. I'm telling you, the home we have now is not the one you knew. I'm sorry to say that, but listen, Kassy . . . in a way, what you've been through—as awful as it has been— is what has caused us to make the changes. It was seeing you all bruised and broken that made me finally stand up to your father."

"I don't understand."

"When I saw you the night Michael died, I realized something. I realized that what I saw as a weakness, even a character flaw in your father, you saw as natural. Your father never beat me, but he did slap me."

"I know."

"And you accepted it as normal. I took it, yes, but I never saw it as normal. I always thought he'd get a handle on it someday. But you—and Jodie even—you had no reason to think your husbands wouldn't slap you. That's when I knew I had to put a stop to it. I didn't want Jodie thinking it was a natural way for a husband to act. And Sammy . . . I didn't want him thinking it was the way you treat a woman." Kate's eyes filled with tears. "I took a risk. I stood up to him and said I wouldn't take it anymore. I said a few other things too, but that's between your father and me." Kate reached for a napkin and wiped her eyes. "I'm telling you, Kassy, your daddy has changed. You won't believe it until you see him. Will you at least see him?"

"I don't know, Mama." Karissa reached across the table toward her mother. "I'll think about it. I really will."

Karissa had no idea she would have such little time to consider seeing her father. Later on that same day he knocked at her front door.

"May I come in and speak with you, Karissa?"

As long as she could remember, her father had never asked her permission to do anything. She was so taken aback, she stepped away from the door and let him pass into the small, tastefully decorated living room. Without a word, she motioned toward a chair and noticed he remained standing until she sat opposite him on the sofa.

"Karissa, I'm afraid I've not been a good father to you. I can't expect you to forget all the times I was entirely too harsh or when I was too strict. All I can say is God has convicted me of how wrong I have been . . . can you forgive me?"

Karissa took a deep breath and shifted uneasily as she felt her unborn child kick her in the rib.

"Daddy," she began, "I don't know . . ." Her eyes dropped to her lap. "I don't know what to . . ."

"You don't have to forgive me this minute. . . . I can wait. You can think about it. Maybe you can't ever forgive me. I don't know. But I wanted to ask. I love you, Kassy."

Karissa couldn't remember her father ever using the family nickname Jodie had pinned on her as a toddler. It seemed everyone in the family had used it from then on—everyone except her father.

"I don't . . ." Karissa found the sudden intimacy uncomfortable. Her mother had said he had changed, but no matter what she had expected, this was more than anything she could have imagined. Karissa stood up and put her hand on her bulging middle. "I don't have any coffee on, but would you like a glass of water, or iced tea?"

"Thanks, but I must be going. I told your mother I'd be there by five forty-five. It's that now. May I use your phone? I'd like to call her."

"Sure," Karissa said, motioning toward the kitchen. "It's in here." It felt strange to have this man in her house. He was familiar—he was her father, after all. But he was different. A man she recognized but felt she didn't even know.

"No, ten minutes, that's all. Is that a problem? Good." Karissa listened to his gentle tone as he talked to Kate. "I love you, sweetheart," he said. Smiling, he replaced the receiver on the telephone. He glanced around the cheerful kitchen and said to Karissa, "Your kitchen feels just like your mother's."

Karissa followed him to the front door. "Daddy?"

"Yes, Kassy?"

"Will you come and see me again?"

"Want me to?"

"Um-hmm. I miss you, Daddy."

"I miss you, too, honey." His eyes filled with tears .

as he reached out to take his daughter's hand and she opened her arms to him. Without hesitancy, Gerald Hill did what he should have done years before— he wrapped his arms around his firstborn.

Suddenly, she felt safer. The baby kicked and Gerry quickly stepped back. "It's okay, little one," Karissa said patting her stomach. "That's just your 'papa.' "

Gerry shook his head as if he couldn't believe it. "I'm really going to be a grandfather," he said, "and I have a two-year-old waiting for me at home. Somehow I thought you'd all grow up and be having babies at the same time. I didn't expect this to happen to me so soon."

"Me either," Karissa laughed. "Me either."

# Twenty-two

Thanksgiving morning Karissa moved around quietly in her kitchen, staying in her robe a little later than usual. After all, she had reasoned, it was a holiday. Running her fingers through her long blond hair, she let it fall where it chose. She actually looked forward to going to her parents' for dinner. She hadn't been around the whole family at once since she married Michael.

The Smiths were coming too, as was Aunt Helen. Karissa looked forward to seeing everyone except stern, strict, proper Aunt Helen.

Finishing her morning glass of milk, Karissa was turning to leave the kitchen when she heard a faint knock on the back door. She secured the belt across her bulging tummy, smoothed her hair behind her ears, and peered out the window to see Holden.

"Good morning," he said as she peeked through a barely open door. "I came home late last night and I have to go back this morning. I need to see you."

"You're leaving again?"

"Just for a few more days. Back to L.A. I might be gone a week, maybe a little longer. It's hard to say." Holden paused and shifted his weight from one foot to another. "May I come in for a minute?"

"Well, I'm not—"

"I promise, I'll only stay a minute."

"Sure. Come on in." Karissa stepped out of his way. "Can I make some coffee?"

"Thanks, but I'll not be staying that long."

"You sure?" Karissa was almost disappointed.

"I'm sure. I only came back because I have something important to ask you and I didn't want to discuss it on the phone. It's not the easiest thing to ask, but . . ." Holden hesitated. It was as if he wanted to say much more but held himself in reserve.

"Sit down for a minute, then," Karissa invited. "Something wrong?"

"I don't think so. But I'm going to find out. Manny Rodriguez, you know him?"

"Sure. He's a friend of Michael's—or was." Karissa looked down at her lap, avoiding Holden's gaze. "I saw him just before . . ."

"I know. Have you seen him since?"

"No. I heard he got a job in the city," she frowned. "Is this why you're going to L.A.?"

"I talked with a detective a few weeks ago. He said they want to talk to Manny about Michael—about the night of the accident. It seems there are some questions in Mr. Walker's mind about Manny and why he disappeared the night Michael . . ."

"Died." Karissa finished Holden's sentence. "I can say it, I really can. Michael is dead." Karissa paused, and Holden waited for her to continue. "You know something? I'm having some trouble . . ."

"Trouble?" Holden said, concerned.

"Well, maybe you can understand this. I am sorry Michael died, of course. But I'm not sorry he's gone." Karissa's eyes filled with tears. "I've not said that to anyone before. But it's true. I guess that makes me a terrible person, doesn't it?"

"Not at all. I understand more than you think I do."

"You do?"

"I heard that Michael gave you quite a beating that night."

"Not just that night."

"How long had he. . . ?" Holden couldn't finish the question.

"A long time."

"But you'd only been married since January, right? When did he start beating you?"

"Sometime in February, I think. He was so frustrated with me for something—I can't remember what it was. But he hit me."

Holden took a deep breath and leaned forward on the kitchen table. "Then what happened?"

"He was sorry. He said it was because he was under such pressure from his parents. He wasn't doing well in college. He wanted to quit and just get a job. Phyllis wasn't too happy with Mark for refusing to hire him. Mark made him stay in school. It didn't do any good. He failed most of his classes anyway."

"So he took it out on you," Holden said.

"Yeah, I guess. I wasn't perfect, though. I knew when he was upset. I tried to help him with his homework. But I had my own to do. He got mad when I couldn't help him."

"He was in college?" Holden asked.

"Yeah, the community college."

"And you were in high school?"

"Yes."

"And he expected you to help him with his homework?"

"It wasn't too hard, really. He was taking business courses. I thought they were interesting. He got mad when I would read his books and try to explain things to him. He thought I was trying to make him look bad."

"So he started beating you soon after you got married. How did he convince you to run away with him in the first place?"

"He said if only we were married, his mother

would get off his back about Laura Wheaton. Phyllis wanted him to marry her. I guess her parents are just about the most important people at the club."

"And Laura?"

"She dated Michael whenever he called, but he said she wasn't his type. Laura is sophisticated . . . she's going to UCLA. Michael thought she was too . . . well . . . I don't know . . ."

"Strong?"

"Maybe. He said she was too much like his mother."

"And Manny? Where does he come into all this?"

"Manny was just about Michael's best friend," Karissa said. "Not like Sandy and I are best friends. But the best one of the whole group. At least I thought so. He was always polite and always smiled at me. He never put his feet on the furniture and was in the kitchen to help me whenever Michael and his friends were over. Michael teased him about wanting to be in the kitchen. One time Michael was drinking and Manny was helping me make hamburgers. Michael came into the kitchen and tried to kiss me in front of Manny—just to let him know whose wife I was."

Karissa winced at the memory of Michael's rough kiss and how tightly he had held her against him with her wrists down and behind her waist.

"Manny stormed out of the kitchen and slammed out the front door. Michael just stood there and laughed, then he dragged me into the living room and proceeded to announce to everyone that I was 'his woman,' as he put it. He didn't want anyone to forget it."

"Manny ever try anything?"

"With me?" Karissa's eyes opened wide. "The most he ever tried was when I was a junior. He was a senior. Michael graduated the year before. We were at the homecoming dance. Manny asked me to dance and Michael said it was okay. Then Michael lined up all his friends and made me dance with every one of them."

"How'd that make you feel?"

"Like a new bike a kid lets the whole neighborhood take turns on." Karissa's tears spilled down her cheeks and she wiped them away with her hand.

"Why'd you marry him?"

"He said he loved me. He could be so nice when he wanted to be," Karissa said. "He said that if we got married, his mother would get off his back and stop pushing Laura at him. He said his father would have to give him a job then and he could quit school. He didn't really think he needed to go to school—he would inherit his father's business someday anyway. Michael thought you only needed to go to school if you didn't know what you wanted to be or if you wanted to be a doctor or teacher or something like that."

"So marrying you was his ticket out of college."

"I guess it was. I thought I could make him happy. I thought that if we were married he would settle down and . . ."

"Change?"

"Yeah."

"Did he change?"

"Yes. He got worse." Karissa's voice was barely above a whisper. "I guess I wasn't a good wife. I thought I could . . ." Karissa left the sentence unfinished. "Am I an evil person?" She looked imploringly into Holden's eyes.

Holden could no longer stay in his seat. He crossed the room and stared out the kitchen window. He wanted to somehow make it right for her. He hadn't felt this way since he had watched his beloved Julie give birth to Kenneth. But then, he had loved only that one time—until now. Now he knew, he had fallen in love with Karissa.

He turned back to look at her sitting at the kitchen table, her hair falling gently about her tear-streaked face. Her pain had become his. He wanted to take her in his arms and hold her until all the pain was gone. He wanted to hold her—because he loved her, not because Michael didn't.

"Karissa," Holden said, his husky voice low and tender, "listen to me. You are not an evil person. You are a young woman who's been very hurt and mis-used. Michael Andrews abused you. You didn't de-serve what he did to you. Thank God he can never hurt you again. You are free of him, Karissa." Holden stepped close to her and took her hands in his. "Please, find a way to put all that pain into the grave with Michael. You have a life to live . . . you have a precious little baby who needs you to be happy."

Holden was surprised to find the words coming so easily. But then he never felt more at ease than when he was with Karissa. At ease, and yet at the same time, in such turmoil. It was too soon to ask her to think of him, Holden knew that. "Think of that little one in there." Holden nodded toward Karissa's tummy. "That little one will never need to be afraid of Michael."

Karissa withdrew her hands from Holden's, stood, and crossed the kitchen to stand at the sink. She stared out into the backyard she had come to love so much. "I know. At least I can be thankful for that." She laid her hands across her stomach. Turning to Holden she said, "Thank you."

"For what?"

"For coming. And for that—" She nodded toward the backyard. "I can't thank you enough for taking care of my yard."

"Well, it's nothing really. It's got potential, though."

"Potential?"

"A trellis or a fountain would really look good in that back corner, wouldn't you say?" Without waiting for an answer, Holden joined her in looking out the kitchen window. Standing near her, he pointed to the side fence. "And I think a gate over there to Aunt Mattie's yard would save you both quite a few steps. What do you think?"

"Wouldn't that be great?" Karissa's eyes twinkled at Holden's ideas.

"And a few patio blocks making a walkway from the gate—not straight but kind of curving across the lawn to your patio."

Karissa turned and looked directly into Holden's eyes. "You're a nice man, Mr. Kelley. The nicest man I ever knew."

Holden turned and faced her. "And you are the sweetest young woman I've ever met," he said. He looked deep into her blue eyes and let his eyes fall to her full, soft lips. "And," he hoarsely whispered, "you're going to be a wonderful mother."

Holden looked at the young, trusting face and leaned forward to plant a soft kiss on Karissa's cheek. Then he quickly stepped back and walked toward the door.

"Karissa," he said, not turning around. "Karissa," he repeated when she didn't answer. Turning around, he saw the tears streaming down her face. "Karissa, listen to me," he said. "I'm only going back to L.A. for a little while. Just to find Manny, that's all. My work there is done and when I find him I'll be back. I'm not sure how long I'll be gone. This whole mess has to be straightened out. It's important to find out what happened to Michael." Holden stepped toward her again. "Like I said, I don't know how long

I'll be gone. But when I get back, you and I need to have a serious talk."

Karissa stood looking at him, motionless. She didn't even move to wipe the tears from her face.

Holden closed the distance between them. "It's been only two months since your husband died. I know that. But I also know you shouldn't have married him. I think that if he hadn't talked you into running away that night, you probably wouldn't have. I don't know for sure, of course. Maybe it's just what I've been telling myself to excuse the feelings I have for you."

"Feelings?" Karissa could barely believe what she was hearing.

"I said . . . when I get back. We'll talk then. But until then, will you think about this—I mean, when I get back, I want us to . . ." Holden's tongue seemed to thicken and he could hardly organize his thoughts. "What I mean, Karissa, is this," he said with firm determination. "I want to see you." He fairly spat the words out.

"You do?"

"Do you?"

"I think so. . . ." Karissa said. "I mean, that would be nice." Karissa's smile broadened, and Holden saw her bright white teeth. She suddenly lowered her head, and her long, soft hair fell forward to cover the faint color spreading up her neck to her cheeks.

Holden tossed his reserve aside and gently pulled Karissa within the circle of his arms. She neither resisted nor responded. Holden touched her forehead lightly with his lips, and ever so slightly, she leaned her head into his gentle kiss. He dropped his arms and backed away.

"I'll be away only as long as I have to. I'll call you soon, okay?"

Karissa nodded as Holden opened the back door

without taking his eyes off her. She didn't move from her position at the kitchen window.

"Well, well, isn't this interesting?"

Holden spun around and stood face-to-face with the voice—Phyllis Andrews.

"A little early for a social call, isn't it? Or, are you just leaving *very* late?"

"Well, well. If it isn't Phyllis Andrews," Holden said.

"Expecting someone else? No, of course not. It's obvious you weren't expecting anyone at all."

"I see you're still the same old Phyllis," Holden quipped sarcastically.

"And what is that supposed to mean?" Phyllis asked.

"Ask anyone in town. They'll tell you," he answered.

"I beg your pardon?"

"I bet you do," Holden retorted, returning his gaze to Karissa. "You all right with all this?" he asked, gesturing toward Phyllis. He wasn't about to move out of the way without Karissa's approval.

"Perfectly," Karissa said.

"With everything?" Holden double-checked.

"Everything." Karissa smiled at him.

Turning to leave, Holden gave Phyllis an exaggerated bow, then tipped an imaginary hat. "Mrs. Andrews," he said politely.

Phyllis shrugged her shoulders and brushed by him into the house without waiting for a further invitation from Karissa.

"Just as I suspected," she began in an accusatory tone. "You're pregnant."

Karissa felt stronger and happier than she could ever remember. Not even Phyllis Andrews could dampen her spirits today. "And come January," she said, "*you* are going to be a grandmother."

Phyllis winced at the thought.

# Twenty-three

Karissa couldn't ever remember enjoying a Thanksgiving more. Holidays had always been tense before, but this one was a joyous family occasion. Karissa was moved almost to tears when Gerry offered his Thanksgiving prayer. Sammy was most enthused about Karissa's "T-bird," and Jodie asked to stay overnight with her sometime.

Karissa excitedly shared the family's good news with Mattie on Friday evening when she went next door for supper. "It's almost as if they've been given a new start," she said. "I can't believe the change in my father."

"New starts are what repentance is all about, my dear," Mattie said. "The Lord doesn't want us to stay stuck in our mistakes and bad decisions. We might live with the consequences, but we can really be free of the pain and regret."

"Do you have any regrets, Mattie?"

"Of course, child. Everyone does."

"I can't imagine you ever doing anything you would have to be sorry for later."

"Karissa, my dear, you have only known me a few short months. But when I was young. . . . Well, I can tell you, the change in my life is as big a miracle as the change in your daddy's."

"I can vouch for that," Ben said from his chair in the corner. "She was quite the wild thing in her day."

"Oh, you. Pipe down. No sense draggin' up old trash, now, is there?"

"She doesn't want you to know what a flapper she was."

"Ben, hold your tongue."

"No kiddin'. I never saw anyone cut a rug like Mattie here. She certainly was what we called the cat's pajamas." Ben laughed as Mattie threw a dish towel his way. "She even won a dance marathon or two."

"Benjamin. Stop it."

"She danced like there was no tomorrow."

"Benjamin, I'm warning you!" Mattie's eyes twinkled, belying her angry tone.

"She danced and made all the guys fall all over themselves. Look at them legs there, still good-lookin' after all these years."

"Now you've pushed me too far, Benjamin Sloan." Turning to Karissa she continued, "Guess who my dance partner was?"

"Go on with you, now." Benjamin hid his face in his paper.

"See, he doesn't want to admit that he was just as guilty of goin' to the speakeasies as I was. Drinkin' and dancin' all night." Mattie's tone softened. "We were just as deep in sin as you could get. Illegal liquor, police raids, corruption—the whole thing. We thought we were havin' a good time, livin' fast and easy."

"What made you change?" Karissa could hardly believe the story this beloved couple told.

"The war," Benjamin said.

"The Lord," Mattie corrected.

"But He used the war, Mama. He certainly used the war."

"That He did, honey."

Karissa had never heard the older couple use such tenderness toward each other before.

Mattie's eyes misted. "You are right. He certainly did use the war."

Karissa listened as Mattie explained the loss she felt when her beloved Benjamin was called into war. She was expecting her first child within weeks of Ben's being shipped overseas to fight for his country.

"I prayed for the first time then." Mattie wiped her nose on the corner of her apron. "And I haven't stopped since." She dabbed at her eyes.

"I came home safe and sound. Lots of others weren't so lucky," Benjamin added. "Then I came home to a sick wife and dying baby."

"It was a hard time," Mattie said.

"Influenza, nineteen and eighteen. Over half a million died. I went all through the war with nary a thought about God or prayer. But when I came home and saw Mattie sufferin' so . . . and the baby so sick . . . I gave both God and prayin' serious attention. Just like Mattie prayed me through the horror of war, I prayed her through the sickness. Our baby, though, didn't make it."

"You know, it's just like Pastor Jim said at Michael's funeral, Karissa. Even in that awful sorrow, God opened a door of hope. While we were laying our little baby in his grave, somehow God was close to us, wasn't He, Ben?"

"Yep. Been close ever since."

"Can't you see Him doin' that with you, Karissa?"

"What do you mean?"

"Your folks, for one thing. Wasn't it after Michael's death that your mama found the strength to stand up to your daddy?"

Karissa nodded.

"And Mark Andrews—hasn't it been because of Michael's death that he took hold of his own responsibilities and affairs?"

"I see what you mean," Karissa said. "The tragedy brought them to their senses."

"Not only their senses, but to recognize their need for God."

"In a way," Karissa said quietly, "Michael's death has been a door of hope for my baby, too."

Mattie reached for Karissa's hand.

"Holden made me see that Thanksgiving morning. He said the baby would never have to be afraid of Michael. In all of this, there really is hope."

"That's because there is a loving God," said Ben. "Karissa, God has been watching out for you. Can't you see that?"

"Ben, I . . ."

"I know I don't speak much, little girl, but listen to me—just this once. I don't talk much about God, but I talk to Him a lot. What I say is between Him and me. I'll never bring it up again, but that little one you're carryin' there needs a mama who knows how to pray. Who knows what growin' up in the sixties will be like. All you have to do is read the paper—you're in for a tough row to hoe, mark my words. You're not just having a baby, Karissa, you're becoming a parent. It's a job too big to try on your own." His speech finally over, Ben disappeared behind his evening paper.

Mattie smiled as much with her eyes as with her mouth. "You heard the old man. He said a mouthful of truth there. He doesn't say much, but when he does, it's worth rememberin'."

———

Back in her own kitchen, Karissa reached for the teakettle, then set it down to answer the phone.

"Hi," Holden's voice greeted her. "It's me."

"How are you? Did you find Manny? What did he say?"

"Whoa! Slow down. I didn't find Manny, well not exactly, anyway. I did find a relative who finally told me he joined the service. He's in boot camp. I called

Walker. He's coming down in the morning. We'll go out to Camp Pendleton tomorrow. That's where Manny is. We should have some answers soon."

Karissa enjoyed listening to Holden's voice on the phone. They chatted for a few minutes, then Holden told her he wasn't coming straight home.

"My dad lives near San Diego. He's not been feeling too well and needs some help straightening out his books and turning them over to a new accountant. I'll only be there a few days at the most. I'll call you as soon as I know anything."

Karissa hung up the phone and reached for a teacup just as Mark knocked lightly on her back door.

"Hi. I was just going to make some tea. I'm glad to see you." Karissa gave her father-in-law a quick hug. "You look tired. You okay?"

"Karissa, did Holden Kelley spend the night here?" Mark was direct.

"What?" Karissa dropped the cup and it shattered on the shiny linoleum floor.

"Phyllis said he was leaving the other morning when she came to see you. She said you were still in your robe. She said she saw the two of you 'making out' in the kitchen." Mark ran both hands back over his head and rubbed his neck at the base of his skull.

"Mark. How could you even think. . . ?" Karissa was dumbfounded. "I can't imagine . . ."

"Well, she can. And she will, given the slightest chance."

"Listen, Mark, Holden is a fine man. A wonderful Christian man. He loves the Lord and he loves his church. Do you think he'd do anything to bring the slightest bit of shame to either?"

"He already did."

"Did what?"

"Phyllis wasted no time in making a few calls. She's really stirred up quite a hornet's nest. She said she confronted the two of you and Holden left town. Is that true?"

Karissa's heart stood still and her eyes filled with tears. "No. Not exactly."

"What do you mean—not exactly?"

"Holden was here Thanksgiving morning. I watched the parade—you know, Macy's parade on TV. It was getting late and I turned off the TV and was about to go take my shower and get ready to go to my parents' for the day. Did you know I went home for Thanksgiving?"

"Your mother told me."

"I was in the kitchen and Holden came to the back door. We talked for a few minutes." Karissa thought about the brief moment when Holden held her in his arms. She had so wanted him to kiss her. Michael had always rushed her, always forced her to kiss him whether she wanted to or not. It was the first time she could ever recall wanting to be kissed. Suddenly, she colored. She didn't want to share those minutes with Mark or anyone. "Was Phyllis spying on me?" Karissa started to cry.

Mark led her to a kitchen chair. "Here, you sit down and I'll sweep up this mess. The water's hot. How about some tea?"

Karissa nodded.

Mark made two cups of tea and grabbed a broom and dustpan from the closet.

"Were you and Holden, you know. . . ?" he asked, sweeping the broken pieces of china into the dustpan.

"Mark! No!" Karissa remembered how close Holden had been and how secure she had felt in his arms. She felt violated by Phyllis's ill-timed visit and her ill-mannered voyeurism. How could Phyllis vulgarize what had happened that morning?

"Listen to me, Kassy. Did Phyllis see anything?"

Mark searched for the right words. "Did she see anything she could have misinterpreted as . . . improper between you and Holden?"

*How could anyone think Holden guilty of anything "improper"?* Karissa wondered.

"Mark, I don't know what to say. . . ." Karissa's cheeks were now wet with her tears. "I'm sorry. I can't talk about this." Karissa stood and moved to the spot where Holden had been so tender to her. "I can't explain . . ."

Mark put the broom away and sat down heavily. "Listen, Karissa, as far as I'm concerned, you couldn't do any better than Holden Kelley. I know him for what he is. My wife, on the other hand . . ." He hesitated, a pained expression on his face.

"What. . . ?"

"She . . . well, she has this idea. It's a crazy idea, Karissa. I don't agree with her. Please know that."

Karissa felt fear begin to grip her insides. "Mark, what are you talking about?" Karissa's voice was barely above a whisper.

"She thinks *we* should raise the baby."

Karissa sat dumbfounded. Her mouth fell open and she pushed her chair back at Mark's words. "I can't believe you would let her say such things. I can't believe you would even—" She ran to the kitchen door and flung it open. "Get out, Mark. Get out of my house!" Karissa's hands began to shake and her body soon trembled uncontrollably.

"Kassy, please don't hate me. I love you, but this is Michael's baby, too. Phyllis says that when you marry, you'll cut us off from the baby. She says—"

"Get out!" Karissa screamed at him as he stood and moved toward her. "Get out of my house! Get out of my life! You can believe her after all she's done to you? Where is your mind?" Karissa shoved Mark toward the door. "How could you even think of such a thing? You think I was doing some awful, immoral thing in the kitchen with Holden Kelley? You think I'd bring shame on him?"

"Karissa, calm down!" Mark tried to hold her still.

"Don't touch me!" she yelled, yanking away from his grasp. Mark sighed deeply, then walked slowly out the door. Karissa quickly locked it behind him, then turned and leaned against it. Wrapping her arms around her unborn child, she sank to the floor and released deep sobs of pain and pent-up grief.

"Don't worry, baby," Karissa finally said as her sobs subsided. "I won't let anyone else be your mama. I'm your mama. Your daddy's dead. But you still have a mama. I won't let anyone come between us. Not Phyllis Andrews"—Karissa started to cry again—"not even Holden Kelley."

# Twenty-four

Holden didn't like the sound of Karissa's voice on the phone when he called early Sunday morning to tell her the police were bringing Manny back to Summerwind for questioning. He had heard the whole story and wanted Karissa to hear it from him instead of Walker, or worse, Phyllis Andrews.

However, when he called, her voice sounded strained.

"I'm just tired today, that's all."

Holden wasn't convinced. "Will you call Aunt Mattie?"

"Maybe later. She's going to church. I'll talk to her later. I'm okay, really. Just tired. Mark came over last night and we talked for a while. I should have gone to bed sooner."

Holden still wasn't convinced. "I'll come back before I go on down to my dad's."

"No." Karissa's tone was insistent. "I mean, really, there's no need. If I don't perk up, I'll call my mother."

Holden decided to wait until he got to his dad's, then he'd call and tell her about Manny's version of Michael's death. He knew Karissa had no idea just how many people were on her side. No idea in the slightest.

———

Across town, Detective Walker sat opposite Manny Rodriguez in a small interrogation room.

"Let me get this straight, Manny. You killed Michael. You sure?"

"I'm positive. Like I told you before, we were all fed up with the way Michael tried to run everything and everyone. He acted like he owned us."

"Who's us?"

"All of us. The guys, you know . . . Jimmy Hernandez, Frankie Jordan, Ricky Martin, and Hank Thomas. Even Bobby Johnson, but he joined the Marines in June." Manny took a deep drag on a cigarette. "We were all fed up to here"—Manny swung his hand above his head—"with Michael Andrews and his high and mighty attitude."

"So you killed him."

"Not just like that."

"What do you mean? He's dead, isn't he?"

"Yeah, but we didn't mean to kill him."

"Oh? And just what did you mean to do?"

"Beat the—" Manny paused and lowered his tone. "We just meant to rough him up a bit. You know, give him a taste of his own medicine."

"His own medicine. Why did you pick that particular night in September? Why not earlier, or wait until Christmas or something?" Walker was impatient to hear what he was pretty sure he already knew.

"Because of Kassy."

"Kassy?"

"Karissa Hill. Mike's gir—his wife."

"What about Mrs. Andrews?"

"Mike beat her that night—right before we all went to the Y."

"Was that the first time he beat her?"

"No. But this was—well, I think it was the worst."

"Why was that, do you think?"

"Mike said she was getting as fat as a pig. But she wasn't. She was just P.G."

"Pregnant?"

"Yeah, Mike strutted all over the place about it at first. He'd even laugh about her throwing up and how sick she was. He was the one who was sick. I hated him for being so cruel to her. Bragging, even. He said he could make Kassy do whatever he wanted, whenever he wanted. Then he said something I'll never forget. He said he could even—" Manny stopped, his composure fragile.

"Could even what, Manny? Then what'd he say?"

"He said he could even make her get rid of it. Lose it, you know, have an accident and . . ."

"So? What'd he do?"

"He beat her. Not so's it would show at first. But then it got worse."

"You know that for sure?"

"We all knew it. But that night was the worst. She looked awful."

"But you say it wasn't the first time he beat her up? When did it start, do you know?"

"Right away, I guess. She never told anyone, though. They got married the night of the January Jubilee—it's sort of a winter prom. A lot of kids get jobs in the groves later, so we have our main high school dance in January."

"She wasn't pregnant then, was she?" Walker already knew the answer to that question.

"Naw—not Karissa. Other girls, maybe, but not her. That didn't happen until sometime in the spring—March, April maybe."

"So you came by the house that night looking for the guys," Walker said.

"Yeah, like I said, we were going to the Y. Frankie had taped the back lock earlier.We did it all the time. We even took girls a few times."

"Ever get caught?"

"Twice. First time, we just got bawled out. Second time, Mike's mother took care of it."

"How'd she do that?"

"Big donation, I guess."

"So you came by the Andrewses' house."

"Yeah, I saw her. She was pretty roughed up. Black eye, twisted ankle. Bruises up and down her arm. He knocked her up, then he knocked her around. That's when we drew straws."

"Straws?"

"Yeah, you know. The short one goes first. Or in this case, the short one got to pull the punch."

"The punch?"

"We decided that the next time he beat Karissa we would beat *him*. There were five of us and we were so scared of him we could only do it in the dark. Two guys held him and I punched him—hard—in the belly." Manny looked tired.

"You want to save the rest until tomorrow?"

"No, I'm glad to finally have it out."

"Then what happened? Where were the other two guys?"

"Standing guard. After I punched him, twice, I left. I almost went back to see if Kassy was okay. But I was afraid that Michael would come home and beat us both. So I just left."

"Where'd you go?"

"Home. I slept in my car. I didn't want my mom to hear me come in."

"Let me get this straight. You all met at the Y and two held him, two stood watch, and you punched him out. You hit him twice."

"Right."

"How do you know you killed him?"

"Because I knocked the wind out of him."

"But he drowned."

"I know. He must have fallen in the water after the guys let go of him."

"Who held him?"

"I'm not sure. It was dark. Pitch dark. Frankie and Hank, I think, but I'm not sure. I know Ricky was by the door—he told us when the coast was clear."

"How do you know you hit Michael, then?"

"I know all right. We planned it. And he was yelling and laughing. He thought we were going to throw him in the water. He thought we were just horsing around."

"But you weren't."

"No, sir. We weren't."

Walker paused for a moment, staring hard at the young man, who shifted uncomfortably in the sudden silence.

"You didn't kill him, you know," Walker went on quietly. "As much as you wanted to, you didn't kill him."

Manny's dark features registered shock and confusion. "How do you know?"

"He drowned because of a blow to his head. He fell into the water, bumped his head, and drowned."

"But I—"

"The other boys talked to him after you left." Walker didn't have the heart to tell Manny that he hadn't hit Michael hard enough to knock the wind out of him. Michael had even made fun of Manny's attempt to defend Karissa.

"But Hank told me that I killed him. That he fell in the water after I hit him, and he never came out."

"Where'd you get friends like this, son? He was up walking around laughing and joking after you left. You didn't kill him . . . you didn't kill anyone." Walker looked at the young man across the table. "Listen to me, Rodriguez, your intentions to defend Mrs. Andrews were noble, but you didn't even phase Andrews. He was drunk—he fell in the pool, bumped his head, and drowned. Michael Andrews killed himself."

"You're telling me it really *was* an accident? And all this time . . ."

"You've been running and hiding for nothing." Walker knew the feeling. Even he had a history he didn't talk about to anyone. "For nothing! You hear me? For nothing. Your friends did you in. Get yourself some new friends, son, okay?" Walker stood and slowly walked to the door. "And go on home. See your mama. Let her hear you come in this time. Tomorrow you go see Karissa Andrews, then you meet me back at the Greyhound station at five sharp. You can get back on base by bed check. And, Manny . . ."

"Yes, sir?"

"Michael Andrews deserved everything he got that night. I might have done the same thing . . . in your shoes."

―――――

Karissa wrapped the pillow around her head until the phone stopped ringing. She knew it was Holden. But she had to think of her baby now, nothing else. There would be no way to avoid him, of course. He was Ben and Mattie's nephew, after all, and he still did her yard. She'd speak to Mark about having him discontinue the service. Her brother Sammy was old enough to help her.

She remembered the ideas Holden had for the yard and how nice the gate would have been between her and Mattie's backyards. She hoped that staying clear of Holden wouldn't mean she'd have to give up Ben and Mattie, too.

But of course, if it meant keeping her baby, Karissa would do anything.

―――――

Phyllis Andrews took a deep breath as she lay in her large, luxurious bed. She had a reason to live again. A new baby was giving it to her.

She knew Karissa would do anything to keep her baby. That was a fact Phyllis counted on—heavily. And if she knew Mark, he'd be putting the rest of the family money in the baby's name almost as soon as it was born. There were still some real estate holdings and, of course, the business. Phyllis wasn't about to let anything come between her and what was left of the Andrewses' money. If she had any control over her financial destiny, it would be necessary to control the destiny of Michael's baby. If anyone could find a way to do that, Phyllis could. She would begin by being the proud, doting grandmother.

Everyone would be so pleased at the club. To think that such a miracle could emerge and lift her from her grief. She'd start first thing in the morning. Her grandchild would have the finest of everything. Thank goodness Mark had finally listened to reason and kept a few charge accounts open to her.

"This calls for a celebration," she said into the darkness and reached beneath the bed for the bottle she kept there for such special occasions. Shaking it, she realized it was almost empty. No matter, there was another in the laundry hamper—just for times like this.

She preferred to share her bed with Mark, but he hadn't slept there in several weeks, maybe even months.

"You're no substitute for my man," she whispered, snuggling her face to the bottle, "but until he comes back, you'll do."

Down the hall, in Michael's old bedroom, Mark tossed on his son's bed. He had checked the level of the bottle beneath Phyllis's bed earlier and the one in the hamper as well. He'd check it again tomorrow. What he would do with the information, though, he didn't know. Somehow it was enough. Just knowing gave him reason enough to stay away from her.

"It wouldn't be like this if I had married someone like Kate Hill," he whispered into the night. Then he shut his eyes tight against the thought of her. He had never chased a married woman, and he wasn't about to start now—and certainly not someone as lovely and good as Kate.

Before he drifted off to sleep, Mark recalled his earlier conversation with Kassy. Phyllis might fear a relationship between Holden and Kassy, but Mark didn't. Smiling into the darkness, Mark determined to make it right with Kassy as soon as possible.

"Dear God," he whispered, "please teach me how to be a good father-in-law to Kassy and how to be a good 'papa' to the baby. I ask you to take control of this area of my life. I don't want to blow it. . . . I need your help desperately."

# Twenty-five

"Good morning, dear." Mattie stood on Karissa's back step and waited for an invitation to come in. She saw that Karissa's blue eyes were swollen and red-rimmed. "You feeling all right?"

"Sure, Mattie. Just a restless night, I guess. Mark came over; we talked too late." Karissa feigned a yawn.

"Well, as soon as you're dressed, Ben has a surprise for you. You know he's been going out to the garage most mornings."

"I know. Remarkable for someone who has as much trouble getting around as he does."

"He's doing much better, in part thanks to you."

"Me?"

"I don't want to spoil his surprise. As soon as you're up and around, come on over. He has a present for you."

Karissa couldn't believe her eyes later when she stood in Ben Sloan's garage. He smiled broadly and pulled back the canvas covering to reveal a crib.

"It was ours," Mattie said. "We used it for our babies, and we had hoped to pass it on to our grandbabies. But as you know, we never had any grandbabies." Mattie wiped her hands on her apron and pulled it up to dab the corner of one eye.

"He sanded it all down, one-handed." Mattie patted Ben's back proudly. Ben's strength and movement had been greatly reduced by the stroke. "Then he varnished it and put on the little decals here." She pointed to three teddy bears holding kite strings.

"It's beautiful, Ben. I don't know what to say. I haven't even begun to think about baby things." Karissa was deeply moved by her elderly neighbor's thoughtfulness. "I can't believe you did this all by yourself."

"A lot of work went into this, my dear," Mattie said.

"And prayers," Ben added. "Prayers for you and that little baby."

"I guess I'll have to put the finishing touches on that small bedroom, won't I?"

"You'll do nothing of the sort. I'm sure we can get Holden to paint whatever is left."

"No." Karissa's answer was short, almost curt.

"But he wouldn't mind. You know, I think he's kind of sweet on you, Karissa."

"Mattie!" Karissa shocked Mattie at the sharpness of her voice. "I mean," Karissa softened her tone, "it's not necessary. Really. There's only a little bit left. The paper is yellow and white stripe. I'll leave that up. Linda Henry said she'd help me whenever I was ready."

"Whatever you say, then." Mattie was puzzled by Karissa's sudden negative attitude toward Holden. She and Ben exchanged puzzled glances.

Ben quickly added, "When the room is ready we'll move it, okay?" Karissa thanked Ben again and made him smile even wider when she kissed him on the cheek before leaving.

Going back into her house, Karissa ignored the ringing phone. As soon as it stopped, she dialed her mother's number. "Hi, I was out in the yard. Did you call?"

After catching up on the family news, Karissa took the phone off the hook and put a pillow over it. Then she busied herself about her small house and yard.

"Karissa, dear." Mattie was once again at Karissa's back door. "Holden's on the phone. He says he's been trying to call you. The phone company says your phone may be off the hook. Will you check?"

Karissa felt her knees shake beneath her. She could no longer avoid talking to him. "I'm sorry, Mattie. It must have gotten knocked off somehow." Being dishonest with her friend didn't make her feel any better. "I . . . I'll make sure it's back on."

Within a few minutes the phone rang and Holden's voice was tinged with irritation. "Are you trying to avoid me?"

"I . . . I don't know what you mean."

"I've been trying to call for hours, Karissa. Are you okay?"

"I'm fine. Didn't Mattie tell you I was?"

"She said you looked tired."

"Come on, I'm pregnant, remember?" Karissa tried to sound irritated, not fearful.

"I wanted to tell you about Manny. He's been—"

"Oh, Holden, there's someone at the door. Will you wait a minute, please?"

Karissa opened the front door to stand face-to-face with Manny Rodriguez.

"Hi," he said.

"Hi," Karissa answered.

"Can I come in?"

"Sure. I'm sorry. Of course, come on in." Karissa opened the door for Manny and left it open in the warm early winter afternoon.

"I don't have much time. I'm catching a bus later back to the base."

"I see."

"Karissa, I'm sorry about Michael. I really thought I . . ." Manny's nearly black eyes sparkled with moisture.

"Manny, can you wait a minute?" Karissa said. "I'm on the phone."

She hurried into the kitchen. "Holden? Manny's here. I have to go. Thanks for calling." She didn't wait for Holden's response before hanging up.

Returning to the living room, she motioned for Manny to sit down in the armchair. *He looks like a Boy Scout, not a Marine*, she thought as she sat down on the sofa. "Nice uniform," she said aloud, trying to put him at ease.

"Thanks."

"Do you like being in the service?"

"I don't know yet. I'm only in basic training. Everybody hates basic."

"Oh, I see."

"Kassy?" Manny began.

"Don't, Manny," Karissa interrupted him. "Don't be sorry for me, okay? I'm doing okay, really. Mark—Michael's dad—has been real nice to me. He sold Michael's big car and bought me a little one. He gives me money now and then to help out until the baby comes."

"Kassy, I have to tell you something." Manny moved to sit beside Karissa on the sofa. "I know you thought I was one of Mike's best friends. But I wasn't."

"You weren't?"

"I saw how he treated you—and what he did to you that night. I couldn't let it happen again."

"What are you saying, Manny?"

"I—I mean we planned to give Mike back some of his own medicine. We waited for him in the Y. When he came in, we punched him out."

Karissa stared at Manny and leaned away from him.

"Don't pull away, Kassy." Manny took her hands in both of his. "I would never hurt you. I watched what Michael did to you, and I hated him for it. Ever since we were in school, I thought you'd get tired of him and his . . . well, you know, how he treated you. I was hoping to be there when you threw him over."

"I don't understand, Manny. You say you and the others beat him up?"

"Well, we only worked him over a bit."

"Did you kill him?"

"No. I thought I did. But Mr. Kelley came to see me. He heard my side of the story and convinced me to tell it to the police. All this time I've been hiding. I finally joined the Marines. And I could have been right here for you. With you."

"*With* me?"

"I'm trying to tell you, Karissa. I love you." Manny pulled Karissa closer and slid himself tight against her.

"Manny, don't. I don't know . . ."

"I know. Mr. Kelley told me."

"What did Mr. Kelley tell you?"

"He said it was too soon for you to be interested in anyone. I just thought that I'd like to tell you how it is with me. That maybe you'd . . ."

Karissa shook her head against the realization of Manny's words. "Don't, please don't."

Karissa began to cry, and Manny moved to kneel in front of her. "Kassy, don't cry. I don't want you to have to cry because of me. I'm leaving. I'll be in the service for four years. You don't have to worry about me. I'll never speak of this again. I promise. Please, don't cry."

"I had no idea, that's all. All I saw was Michael. All I knew was that I failed him. I didn't know you felt this way."

"Would it have made a difference?"

"No. I was Michael's wife."

"Remember the homecoming dance when I asked you to dance?"

"Yes, I do. You were so sweet."

"No I wasn't. Michael punished you because of that, didn't he?"

"He thought—"

"I know what he thought—and I hated him from that night on," Manny confessed. "Later, he asked me if I wanted to . . . well, you know." Manny's eyes begged Karissa to understand.

"He what?"

"I wondered how long it would be before someone would take him up on his offer."

Karissa's face burned with embarrassment.

"You're better off without him, Kassy. Believe me, you're much better off."

Manny stood and offered his hand to help Karissa from the sofa.

"Thank you for coming, Manny," she said. "I really appreciate knowing this. Somehow it helps to know that someone cared, even then."

Karissa moved to give him a quick hug, and Manny suddenly met her mouth with his own. Before she could pull away, Phyllis's presence filled the room.

"Well now, you do get around, don't you? My son's hardly cold in his grave and you have not one, but two suitors. And the baby, is it really Michael's? Oh, well, it will have his name at least." She gave a tug at her long leather gloves. "Tell me, my dear, do you really think after what I've seen here in this house, with my own eyes, any court will believe you're a fit and moral mother?" Phyllis pulled off her long gloves and slapped them against the palm of her hand.

"Phyllis, I didn't hear you come in. . . ."

"Obviously."

"Kassy, I have to go. I'll get in touch soon." Manny

started toward the doorway.

Karissa hated to see him go, but she didn't want him involved with Phyllis's accusations either.

"Thanks for coming, Manny. And, thanks for . . . well, you know, what you did for me."

Karissa watched as Manny walked quickly from her house to the curb. He turned once, waved, and disappeared down the street.

"That was disgusting." Phyllis paced the living room that seemed to close in on Karissa whenever the woman was there. "Just disgusting. And after all the bragging I did to my club this morning!" Phyllis settled herself primly at the end of the sofa.

"Do you want something, Phyllis?" Karissa stood, both hands resting on her hips.

"Don't stand that way, dear. It makes you look even bigger than you are." Phyllis glanced over at Karissa's stomach. "How big are you, anyway? I mean how far along are we, little mother?"

"Eight months." Karissa ignored Phyllis's royal "we."

"Let's see, that means the baby's due in . . ."

"January."

"That means you were probably pregnant at the wedding reception."

"Yes, but not before I was married."

"Oh really?" Phyllis's eyes narrowed. "Not before?"

"Even you can count, Phyllis. We were married in January and the reception wasn't until after graduation, remember? If I was pregnant when I got married, I'd have had this baby by now."

"You can't really blame a mother for asking—you'll understand someday. It's just that I can't help but wonder if that's how you got Michael to run off with you that night. Did he think you were pregnant?"

"No, he didn't."

"Well, I guess I'll never know for sure."

Karissa excused herself to answer the phone. "Phyllis is here, I can't talk now," she said.

"I see." Holden sounded angry. "Shall I call back later?"

"I don't think so, no," Karissa said flatly. "I have quite enough to deal with at the moment. I'd like to be left alone." She hung up the phone and returned to Phyllis.

"If you don't mind, Karissa dear, I'd like to look at the small bedroom."

"What for?"

"Because I just ordered new furniture for our baby, that's why." Phyllis sounded offended.

"I don't want it."

"What?"

"I don't want the furniture. I have a crib coming and I will use whatever other furniture I have. Cancel the order."

"Oh, my dear, I can't do that."

"I don't want the furniture, Phyllis. I'll refuse it when it comes."

Phyllis chose another approach. "Listen, Karissa. Why don't you give up this house. Come live with Mark and me. There's more than enough room. We can give you Michael's room and the baby can have the nursery. You know, I never had the heart to call that room anything else. I brought Michael there as a baby. It would be wonderful to bring *his* baby home there. Don't you think so?"

"No, I don't. Michael was five when you moved there. He wasn't a baby."

"He was *my* baby, Karissa. Until the day he died."

"I know."

Phyllis paused at Karissa's sarcastic remark, then turned to her before leaving. "Think it over, my dear.

I'm telling you, I have enough on you in just a few days to take that baby away from you forever." She smiled sweetly. "But I don't want to do that. I'd much rather see us together as a family. Wouldn't you?"

Phyllis turned and, before Karissa could answer, walked out the door.

"That woman!" Mattie's voice behind Karissa startled her.

"Mattie, you scared me to death!"

"I'm sorry, dear. But Holden is so worried about you. When I saw Mrs. Andrews' car parked out front, I let myself in the back without knocking. What's going on?"

"Oh, Mattie, I don't know what I'm going to do," Karissa burst into tears. "She makes me so mad and scares me out of my wits at the same time." Karissa shot a furtive look at the ringing phone. "That's probably Holden again. I can't talk to him now, Mattie."

Mattie stepped back into the kitchen to answer the phone. "Hello?" She looked back at Karissa through the doorway and smiled. "Yes, Holden, she is all right. Just a few family stresses at the moment. I think we'll have to put our heads together on this one." Mattie shifted from one foot to the other. "No, dear, I don't think that would be a good idea. You take care of your father's business. We'll manage things here."

After a pause Mattie continued. "Not just now, she needs a little time. Let her work this out in her own way, okay? Uncle Ben and I will be right here." Mattie listened for a moment. "Yes, that is always a possibility. Let me do a little praying about that one, okay? Give her a little time, will you, dear?" Mattie looked at Karissa's inquisitive expression. "Oh, I'd say a week or two might be enough. Now, Holden, don't be so impatient." After a few more words that didn't make sense to Karissa, Mattie replaced the receiver softly in its cradle and walked back into the living room.

"You know, Kassy, Phyllis is right about one thing."

"She is?"

"It might not be a bad idea if you lived with someone for a while." Mattie's eyes sparkled with mischief.

"But I have my little house."

"And no income, I hear?"

"I still have a little left from Mark."

"And then what?"

"I have no idea."

"So then, why don't you come and stay with Ben and me?"

"Oh no, I couldn't do that."

"And why not?" Mattie stuck her little chin high in the air, defying Karissa to find a reasonable excuse.

"What about when the baby comes?"

"We love babies. You know that!"

"It might be a good idea, Karissa." Kassy spun around to see Mark standing in the doorway to the kitchen.

"Mark! How long have you been standing there?" she asked, visibly shaken.

"I just let myself in the back. Sorry . . . I didn't mean to startle you. I take it Phyllis was here, wasn't she? I saw her driving away from this direction on my way here."

"Mark, I . . ."

"Don't, Kassy. Let me talk first, okay?"

Karissa's eyes filled with tears. She dropped her gaze, hoping Mark didn't notice.

"The other day, when we—well, when we talked— I've been thinking about what you said and realized I didn't explain myself very well. I have no intention of letting Phyllis get her hands on your baby. It's not the baby anyway. . . ."

"It's not?"

"No, dear Karissa, it's the money."

"The money? What money? There's no money, Mark. I swear. I only have the little you've given me. Oh, don't get me wrong. I'm grateful, it's just that I don't know what to do when that's gone."

"There's more money, Kassy," Mark said. "Oh, it's not money you can write a check for or withdraw from a savings account. It's in investments, real estate, and in the business."

"What's that got to do with me or the baby?"

"The baby is our only heir, Kassy. Don't you realize that? Phyllis is afraid I'll put the entire family estate in the baby's name and she'll not be able to control the money unless she controls the baby."

"Good grief!" Mattie exclaimed. "She has barely enough money for groceries and that woman's trying—"

"Trying is far from succeeding, Mattie," Mark said.

"Then give her the estate, Mark." Karissa moved toward him in sudden openness and Mark held out his arms to his daughter-in-law. "I only want peace for me and my baby." Karissa fell into Mark's arms. "We don't need a lot of money. I never had any before; I'll get along. Besides, if this is what money does to people, I don't think I want my baby near it anyway."

"This isn't what money does to people," Mattie said. "This is what people do to themselves over money."

"Mattie is right, honey. My parents were wonderful people. They had plenty of money. They were generous, thoughtful, and kind people who knew not only how to live well, but the responsibilities that came with their good fortune." Mark paused and stepped away from Karissa. Thoughtfully, he gazed out the window again. "I can't let her have it, Kassy. It would somehow contaminate all that my parents stood for and believed in. Within the past weeks, my parents' values and beliefs have become more important to me than ever before. I have to put the estate's assets, or what's left of them, somewhere where there's no possibility of her ever being able to get her hands on them. I need to get them out of my name so that should there be a divorce, she'd be unable to get control of what my parents worked so hard to get." Turning to Karissa, he once again pulled her within his embrace.

"Please, Kassy, understand. I not only have a responsibility to the family business, but to the baby. It really was Michael's responsibility, but Phyllis would have controlled him the rest of his life. It's hard for me to say this, but, really, Karissa—as painful as this has all been, you really will be better off without him. And"—Mark took a deep breath—"so will the baby."

Karissa snuggled her head beneath Mark's chin. Silently, she closed her eyes against the painful truth that she had fought against admitting. "I can't let her near the baby, Mark. I just can't."

"I know, sweetheart, I know."

"So what am I going to do?"

"Come live with Ben and me!" Mattie said cheerfully.

"You know, Kassy, it could be just the right answer. You can't go home, you know that for sure?"

"Yes, I'm sure. My parents are working out their own problems. Besides, there's no room."

"So then, you wouldn't have to sell the house. You could wait until after the baby comes to make such a big decision. You could rent it out and have a steady income."

"And," Mattie added, "you'd have chaperons. What could Phyllis Andrews possibly complain about then?"

"Can I sleep on it?" Karissa asked.

"Of course," Mark and Mattie agreed.

"You know, that upstairs of mine could use a good cleanin'. You know anyone who might be able to help?" Mattie asked Mark.

"Maria," Mark said as a smile crossed his face. "I cut her hours at the house. I know she would be glad to have the extra money. I'll call her first thing tomorrow morning."

Karissa shook her head. "I thought I was going to sleep on it, but it's obvious you two know what I'm going to do."

"Not so." Mattie winked at Mark. "We only know what we *hope* you'll do."

Karissa was fairly certain Holden would like it as well. And she was absolutely positive Phyllis Andrews would be furious. Somehow that made the decision easier.

"Mark?" Karissa said.

"Yes."

"I'm sorry."

"Sorry?"

"If you two'll excuse me," Mattie said, "I'll go tell Ben the good news. He'll be delighted."

"Mattie, I am going to sleep on it, remember?" Karissa laughed.

"You sleep—Ben and I'll pray," Mattie tossed over her shoulder as she went out the back door.

"Great, the two of them teaming up with God against me. Fat chance I have of making my own decision."

"They love you, Kassy. And so do I—like my very own daughter." Mark smiled at the young woman.

"I know you do, Mark. And that's why I'm so sorry. I didn't mean to be so—"

"You don't have to say any more. I was way out of line the other day. I have made some serious decisions since our argument."

Karissa found a comfortable spot on the sofa and Mark took the chair facing her. "What kind of decisions?"

"Decisions about Phyllis, about me, you—the baby." Mark paused, took a deep breath, and closed his eyes momentarily before continuing. "But most of all, I have decided to commit my life—or what's left of it—to Christ. I don't know if I'll do very well at this Christian stuff. But I'm going to give it a try. It worked for my folks, and I just hope it's not too late to work for me, too."

Mark looked for some kind of understanding in Karissa's expression. She avoided meeting his gaze.

"Kassy, look at me." Mark waited while she found the courage to meet his eyes with her own. "Look, honey, you and me and the baby—well, the way I see it, we're family. You're my son's wife. That baby you're carrying is my grandchild—my *only* grandchild. I'd do anything for you and the baby. Phyllis, well, she's . . ." Mark searched for the right words. "Let's just say that she's not going to come between us ever again. Marrying you was the only decision Michael ever made without his mother's permission. I must say, for all his faults, his only independent decision was a good one. I couldn't ever want more in a daughter-in-law than I have in you, Kassy."

Karissa's tears found their way down her cheeks and plopped, unchecked, into her lap. "Oh, Mark . . ." She sniffed and wiped her wet cheeks with her hand.

"I mean it, Kassy. Since Michael's death, you have been more of a daughter to me than he ever was a son. It wasn't his fault, really. I should have stood up to Phyllis long ago. Mistakes have been made that I will regret for the rest of my life." Mark moved to sit beside her on the couch. "Kassy"—Mark took her hands in his own—"let's make our little family a good one, shall we?"

"I want that, too, Mark. I really do. I don't want to have this baby all alone. I have my mother, of course. But she and my dad, well, they're working out their problems right now. I don't want to burden them."

"You're not a burden, Karissa. I know both your parents well enough by now to know that. They have been caught off guard by all of this, too. What has happened to you has made us all stop and take a second look at our own lives. You'll see—mark my words—good will come of this for all of us. Sad, isn't it?"

"What?"

"It took something as tragic as losing my son to make us all aware of changes we needed to make. In some ways, the sorrow of his death really opened a door of hope. I can't explain it really. . . ."

"I can."

"You can?"

"Look at this." Karissa produced a worn three-by-five card from the table at her side. "Pastor Jim gave it to me at the funeral." She handed the card to Mark.

Mark read silently, then barely above a whisper he said, ". . . the valley of Achor for a door of hope. . . . What's that mean?"

"Jim said something about sorrow often being a door of hope."

"Is there hope for us, Kassy?"

"Of course there is. Hope for all of us." Karissa felt the baby kick against her ribs. "See?" she laughed, putting her hand on her stomach. "Even the baby says so."

# Twenty-six

Phyllis Andrews slammed the door behind her as she entered Mark's small office. "I suppose you're behind this?"

"Hello, Phyllis."

"You knew about this all along."

"Can I get you something to drink? Theresa, bring Mrs. Andrews a cup of coffee, will you?" Mark said into the intercom. "No, black will be fine. Thanks."

"How could you let this happen?"

"It's good to see you out, Phyllis. And sober, I assume?"

"Listen, Mark, she's moving in with those neighbors of hers. That old couple."

"How are you feeling, dearest?" Mark asked sarcastically.

"She's been planning it for weeks. You knew all along, didn't you?"

Mark rested his chin in his palm. "I have an important appointment in ten minutes, Phyllis. Make this tirade short, will you?"

"If I could ever talk to you at home I wouldn't have to come all the way down—here." Phyllis looked around at Mark's modest office with disdain. She liked the former location on Center Avenue better.

"I like this office, Phyllis. It's street level, it's got a window, even. Not much of a view. . . ." Mark pulled back the drapery that covered the view of the railroad tracks running across the landscape. "But it's cheap, it's serviceable, and it's mine. I decorated it myself. Didn't take much work, though. I vacuumed the carpet and dusted the windowsill. That's about all."

"Mark . . ." Phyllis was intensely frustrated. "Karissa is taking our baby into the home of strangers."

"Wrong."

"Wrong?"

"It's not *our* baby and the Sloans aren't strangers."

"It's so she can be near *him*, that disgusting gardener of hers. You hired him, didn't you? Another one of your disastrous mistakes."

"Wrong again. He's not a gardener, he's not disgusting . . . and he's one of my better decisions," Mark said with a smile.

"I don't understand you, Mark Andrews." Phyllis was clearly agitated by this last remark. "Can't you see we've got to do something about this?" Phyllis paced back and forth in Mark's office.

"Mr. Reynolds to see you." Theresa's voice came clearly across the intercom.

"Jason Reynolds?" Phyllis was immediately interested.

"I'll be with him momentarily, Theresa." Mark looked at his wife. "It's time for you to go, Phyllis."

"How could you let Jason Reynolds come to this dump?" she fairly shrieked.

"Are you leaving or not?"

"I think you could at least make pleasantries."

"You mean introduce you."

"I *am* your wife, Mark."

"I remember." Mark grabbed his jacket. "Are you leaving or am I?"

"Are you going to introduce me?"

"Will you leave then?"

"I'll leave just as soon as I'm sure he won't feel like I've cut him off."

"Fine, let's go."

"Go?"

"You wouldn't want him being *sent* into my office, now, would you?"

"Of course. You're right, you should meet him in the outer office. I'll wait here."

"Good. I'll just spruce up a bit." Mark tightened his tie and put on his coat. "How do I look?"

Phyllis passed her eyes over his suit. "I do wish you'd not buy ready-to-wear. It's so—"

"Affordable." Mark's answer cut her off quickly.

"Your appointment is waiting," Theresa's voice came over the intercom.

"You'll wait right here, then?" Mark asked.

"Right here. I promise." Phyllis flashed Mark a winning smile.

Mark left the office and stepped into the receptionist's area. He closed the door quietly behind him, but the walls weren't thick enough to prevent Phyllis from hearing their greetings.

"Hey, good to see you, Mark. It's been a long time."

"How's life been treating you, Jason?"

"Can't complain, can't complain."

Mark spoke a few words to Theresa—probably ordering fresh coffee or even a cocktail, Phyllis thought. She licked her dry lips and posed sweetly on the overstuffed leather sofa she had so carefully chosen for Mark's other office. Maybe meeting Jason Reynolds here in Mark's office would quell the rumors that his wife Mindy was spreading about her and Mark having problems. She relished the idea of looking like the adoring wife and making Mindy look like a fool.

After waiting a moment or two, she heard the outside door close. She got up and tiptoed to the door and opened it a slight crack. Nothing. No sounds, no men's voices. Only Theresa's noises as she put another sheet of paper in the typewriter.

Creeping out, Phyllis peeked around the corner. "Psst." Theresa looked up without a word.

"Where'd they go?" Phyllis whispered.

"To the site," Theresa whispered back.

Phyllis stormed back into Mark's office and grabbed her purse and coat from off the sofa. She stomped to the doorway, and then returned to pick up the cup of coffee Theresa had brought in, and threw it against the wall behind Mark's desk.

As she walked quickly past Theresa's desk, Phyllis caught the secretary's astonished look out of the corner of her eye. Slamming the door behind her, she muttered under her breath, "Let her think whatever she wants. Let them *all* think whatever they want!"

———————

Karissa and Kate had helped Maria carefully prepare the upstairs rooms for Karissa and the baby. It had been some time since Mattie and Ben had used those rooms to live in; for years they had been neglected, used as a storage area for a growing collection of things. They carted boxes of family pictures, old Christmas decorations, and assorted junk into the garage, where Mattie could sort it at her leisure.

Finally the rooms were clean, ready for the painters to come and finish the task. Ben had insisted on hiring it done, even though Kate and Karissa assured him they could have done it as well and for less money.

"Money! What's that?" he had exclaimed. "When I'm gone I want my house left in good repair behind me. Money does nobody no good just sittin' there when it could be put to good use."

"No use, girls," Mattie told the two, who looked more like sisters than mother and daughter. "Once the old codger makes up his mind, there's no talkin' him out of it."

"Just pick your color. That's all the harder I want you to work," Ben said.

"*Now* you tell me. After I carried all those boxes of your old junk to the garage," Karissa teased.

"That's not junk, it's stuff! Good stuff!" Ben laughed. Karissa smiled at the adoring look Mattie gave her husband.

"Holden's coming this weekend. He'll want to inspect the work so far," Mattie announced. "He wants to see you as well—he said he wants to talk to your dad first, then he'll be calling you for a real date."

Karissa shot her mother a fearful look.

"It's okay, honey. You can't take a mother's baby away because she chooses to get on with her life. After all, you're young yet."

Somehow Karissa knew Phyllis wasn't about to give up easily. But the prospect of living with Ben and Mattie made her feel safer. She'd be moving in with them by the end of the month. The new tenants who would be renting her house had welcomed the furniture she couldn't use at the Sloans. Phyllis was outraged, of course.

———

On Wednesday evening Holden called. "I talked to your father this morning," he said.

"You did?"

"I would have preferred to talk to him face-to-face, but he understood why I had to call. I asked him if I could court you, Karissa."

Karissa's stomach tightened with excitement. "What did he say?"

"He said he trusted your judgment. He asked only that I treat you with respect and that I not hurry you into a relationship you might not be ready for. Do you feel like I'm rushing you?"

"No, I don't. I'm glad you called him. I really do love my dad."

"And he loves you, do you know that?"

"I'm learning."

"So then, how about it?"

"How about what?"

"May I take you out Friday evening?"

"Yes," Karissa said softly. "Yes, of course."

Later that evening, when Karissa called Kate to tell her of Holden's invitation, she suddenly realized that her wardrobe was severely limited. She had borrowed a few of Kate's old maternity clothes for everyday wear, but they certainly were not appropriate for her first real date with Holden. Looking in her closet, Karissa laughed at the clothes she had been wearing just a few months earlier—the full-skirted cotton shirtwaist dresses and the layers of crinoline petticoats that had been so carefully stiffened with sugar water each week and stretched and pinned upside down under all four clotheslines in the backyard to dry. It was a ritual necessary in order to fill her skirts out as full as possible. As she dug through the closet, she listened to the radio for company. Pat Boone's soft voice crooning "love letters in the sand" reminded her of her senior prom last January. Now that night seemed more like a decade ago.

"Mama, what am I going to wear?" Karissa fairly cried into the phone.

"Well, my dear, we'll have to buy you a special dress for the occasion."

"But, Mama, maternity clothes cost so much—and I'm not going to need them much longer. If we had more time we could make one. But what am I going to do now?"

"Let me talk to your dad. Maybe we've got a little extra and . . ."

"No. I think I have enough saved away. Mark says I have to be careful, but when he says to be careful and when we say be careful—we're not talking the same language. Know what I mean?"

Kate and Karissa made plans to go shopping the next morning, leaving Kate's preschoolers with Sandy's mother for a couple of hours. They found a beautiful dress in a soft pink chiffon that draped elegantly on Karissa's full figure.

Karissa carefully checked the receipt. "Almost twenty dollars. I don't know, Mama. . . ."

"I hardly think you've broken the bank, Kassy. And just look at what a beautiful dress you have for the occasion. And who knows? Maybe someday you'll wear it again."

Karissa colored. "Really, Mama. He only asked me for a date, not marriage."

"Where's he taking you?"

"To dinner, that's all I know."

———

Karissa was carefully dressed and waiting when Holden at long last knocked on her door. She had styled and restyled her hair, painted her nails a soft pink, and tucked her tube of Tangee lipstick in her purse next to a pocket-sized package of tissue. In her excitement she almost forgot to take her house keys but caught sight of them on the table just before shutting the door. Once she was settled beside Holden in his car, she felt a little calmer.

Holden had decided to take her to a Chinese restaurant, a new experience for Karissa. She was captivated by the hanging paper lanterns and the large porcelain spoons served with the egg drop soup. She bravely sampled the exotic appetizers, grateful that her tummy wasn't nearly as touchy as it had been a few months earlier.

"Where's the silverware?" she asked quietly.

"There's no silverware," Holden said, a twinkle in his eye.

"No silverware? How are we supposed to eat our food?"

Holden unwrapped the tissue from around his pair of chopsticks and placed them expertly between his fingers. "Like this," he said, easily lifting a bite-sized piece of sweet and sour pork to his lips.

Karissa tried to mimic Holden's hold on the long, slender wooden sticks but couldn't seem to make them spread apart and then close around her food. After several unsuccessful attempts, with food falling back onto her plate, she stabbed impatiently at the pieces of meat on her plate. Holden seemed to fully enjoy watching her struggle. Finally he reached forward and began to feed her with his own chopsticks.

"More tea?" the lovely Oriental waitress asked. She bent over the table and poured more hot, steaming liquid into Karissa's cup. At the same time, Karissa felt something cold and hard pressed into her hand. She knew at once what it was.

"Thank you," Karissa said, smiling at the young woman not much older than herself. Holden sat back until the waitress left their table, then took a bite of his own food. Waiting for just the right moment, Karissa produced the secreted fork and happily began to eat her dinner.

"Hey, that's not fair!" Holden laughed out loud.

Karissa thought it one of the most wonderful sounds she had ever heard.

---

"You want to come in?" It had been a most enjoyable evening and Karissa hesitated to let it come to an end.

"I can't." Holden securely planted both feet on the back step.

"I can stay out for a while longer," Karissa said and watched as a gentle smile tugged at his generous mouth.

"Don't you think you might get cold?"

"I'll get a jacket."

"You think you'll need it?" he teased.

"I'll get my jacket." Karissa felt the irritating flush creep up her neck.

Out in the backyard, Karissa asked Holden to repeat his ideas for the yard.

"Does it matter now?"

"It does to me. I think it's fun to plan and think of making gates and paths."

"Well, then, madam. Let me tell you a few more of my ideas." Holden walked around in the semidarkness and explained to Karissa how an English flower garden was laid out. He pointed to a little side yard and indicated rows of vegetables and herbs. Karissa pulled her jacket up around her chin, growing silent as Holden talked on.

"Something wrong, Kassy?"

"Not really. I was just thinking what a shame it is that this will never happen. My yard, my own yard. It's going to be hard living right next door and not being able to come out here."

Holden closed the distance between them. Gathering Karissa close in his arms, he whispered, "Don't you worry, honey. Phyllis Andrews can't ruin what we have growing between us. I promise you that." Holden ducked his head to touch Karissa's face with his own and discovered the tears silently streaming down her cheeks. One by one he gently kissed them away.

"Karissa Andrews, I love you."

"Oh, Holden, I can hardly believe it. But I love you too."

And then, on a crisp California December night, Holden Kelley kissed her like she had only dreamed it could be.

Back in her bedroom, Karissa took the chopsticks Holden had fed her with out of their paper napkin hiding place and tucked them safely into her dresser drawer—right beside her cherished Bible promise card.

———

The phone rang the moment Holden was inside Mattie's back door.

"It's Mercy Hospital, Holden." Mattie's face was pale and Holden knew immediately—his father was dead.

"I have to go," Holden told Mattie.

"I know you do," Mattie said. "Don't worry about Karissa; we'll keep close watch over her."

Karissa was as understanding as Mattie and came immediately when Holden called. She walked him to his car and he held her for a long moment before he lifted his face from the softness of her hair. "I have only one regret with my dad, Karissa. Only one." He looked into the face of his beloved Karissa Andrews. "He didn't get to meet you. The person who brought life back into my heart."

"I thought God did that," Karissa said.

"He gave me hope, sweetheart, but you brought it to life."

Karissa watched Holden drive away as she stood bundled in her jacket at the curb. She couldn't remember loving anyone or anything this much. She rubbed her stomach. Even walking seemed to be getting harder each day. A stab of pain in her lower back momentarily took her breath away.

"Hang on there, baby, you still have four weeks to go!" Karissa walked slowly toward the house. "Let's at least get through the holidays, okay?"

# Twenty-seven

With Holden away taking care of his father's affairs, Karissa felt suddenly lost. She began to sort and pack away her things and realized that hardly anything in the house fit the criteria her mother gave—if you didn't pick it out, or if it isn't something you would choose, sell it or give it away. Those things that she would have picked for herself, she would pack carefully and store in the garage. She hadn't offered garage privileges with the house.

In spite of Phyllis's protests, Karissa either sold, gave away, or left behind most of Phyllis's hand-me-down furniture. Mark kept her at bay as much as he could, but his new project with Jason Reynolds was coming together quickly and it required most of his attention. Phyllis tried to make the most of the situation by putting on a generous facade to the social circle that meant so much to her.

"It's really nothing I'd want back anyway," she said when Karissa sold the sofa and matching chair. "The tables would soon need refinishing, and I'm sure the child knows nothing about it—it's best she sell it." But inside, Phyllis was livid. She had given Michael and Karissa those things so that Michael would have a decent place to live. She hadn't trusted Karissa to know quality or to select furnishings that suited Michael.

The sunburst clock went to Ned and Margie Smith. Jim and Linda were more than happy to get the extra set of everyday dishes. Only the barest essentials were stored for Karissa in case she ever decided to set up her own little home again. For now, all she wanted to do was be rid of anything that reminded her of Michael. Her life with him, as short as it was, was now past. Karissa looked forward to a whole new future. She prayed each night that Holden was a big part of that future. Thinking about Holden's comments concerning friendship with God, she also prayed, "I don't know why you'd pick me to be your friend, dear Father, but if you can see any hope for us to be closer, I'd sure like to try."

Karissa had agreed to take her mother Christmas shopping, but finding it increasingly difficult to get behind the wheel of the little car, she was just as glad to leave the driving to Kate.

By the time Christmas was over, Karissa was completely settled in the little upstairs rooms at the Sloans. They were delighted to have her and treated her like the granddaughter they never had. They were becoming quite fond of Kate as well.

Karissa and Holden contented themselves with just being together whenever he could get back to town. Taking care of his father's business had become quite a challenge. The elder Holden Kelley had started a number of jobs that needed close supervision. Holden's presence was critical because the profit made on the jobs was the only way to leave his father's business solvent. In the past few years, Holden Sr. had risked far too much and borrowed far too heavily to finance his work. Holden's own projects in Summerwind had come to completion and he was now free to attend to the family business—except for Karissa. The hold she had on his heart kept him tied to Summerwind like his business never had.

"I don't understand," Karissa said to Mark on the afternoon of New Year's Eve as they sat with Mattie and Ben in their living room. "Why can't he just hire the jobs out and come on back? Surely there are other gardeners there who would love to take over for him."

"You don't understand what it is that Holden does, do you?"

"Don't I? I mean, I've seen him work in my yard and in Ben and Mattie's. He got someone to take them over while he's gone. Can't he do that down there?"

Mark laughed and pulled Karissa closer. "Listen, little mother, your Holden Kelley isn't a gardener. He's one of the most talented landscape architects in the whole five-county area."

"He's what?" Karissa's mouth fell open.

"His father was an artist when it came to landscape. His projects included designing the gardens surrounding the county buildings, the governor's mansion, and the formal garden at the city park." Mark had noticed the same unusual artistry emerging in Holden Jr.'s work, as had several others. "Some of the wealthiest people in the southern part of the state are Kelley Corporation clients. Right now, Holden is supervising the courtyard of one of the classiest shopping areas in all of California. His father designed it and died before it was finished. Holden Sr. didn't leave his son a business, but a legacy. How Holden finishes it is not only a memorial to his father, but the establishing of his own career and reputation."

"I didn't know." Karissa's eyes clouded. "There's so much I don't know about him. Why didn't he tell me?"

"He's a modest man, Karissa. Extremely modest. And one of the most talented I have ever met in my whole life. He's got his head on straight, that one. His heart's pure and his life's a testimony to what a

Christian is supposed to be. His personal as well as his professional reputation is spotless."

Karissa stirred beside her father-in-law.

"What's the matter, Kassy?" Mark asked.

"Just uncomfortable, that's all. I'm not used to being so big. I feel like a cow. I'm just as glad Holden isn't coming back for New Year's. I'll probably just go to bed early."

Mattie and Ben exchanged knowing looks. Holden was already on his way. It was early in the evening yet, and he didn't expect to arrive until around nine o'clock. His coming was intended to surprise Karissa.

"How much longer until my grandchild comes?" Mark asked.

"In two or three weeks, according to the doctor. But I'm not really sure when . . ." Karissa's face grew sober, and Mark decided to rescue her.

"Listen, that baby will come whenever it's ready. Not a moment too soon, not a minute too late." Mark stood to leave and motioned Karissa to stay where she was.

"We're going to the club tonight—as usual," Mark said. "Whether or not I want to. I'd rather attend the service at church. You going?"

"I don't think so. Linda offered to pick me up, but I'm tired. Ben and Mattie and I have decided to make a new tradition—we're going to snore in the New Year." Karissa shifted again. "My folks are going, though."

"How are they doing?"

"It's a miracle, Mark. I've never seen anyone change as much as my dad has. He worships the ground my mother walks on. I think he always did, but now he shows it. She couldn't be happier and neither could he."

"Is he moving home soon?"

"Can you keep a secret?"

"Sure."

"He's taking her to church tonight and Jim is going to have them repeat their vows. They don't want anyone to know, but since you're not going anyway, I don't think it hurts for you to know."

A slight frown creased Mark's forehead, but then he smiled quickly. "That's really nice, Kassy."

"Then you know what they're doing?" Karissa went on. "They're going on a little honeymoon. Sandy is staying with the kids. I would, but you can see I'm in no condition to chase Lisa around. I think Dad is taking Mom to the beach. They'll be back day after tomorrow."

"I'm happy for them," Mark said quietly. "I really am."

Karissa noticed how his shoulders sagged as he walked to the door. "I guess I'd better get going. My tux is hanging on the closet door just waiting for me. At midnight, I'll drink a toast to your folks, okay?"

"And a little prayer?"

"I'll see what I can do. The country club isn't the place you'd choose to pray in the New Year. I just hope Phyllis is still sober by then."

Karissa watched him go out and close the front door. She didn't move from her place on the couch. Her back ached. The baby had been quiet all day. Too quiet. She wondered if everything was all right but didn't mention it to Mattie—she didn't want to worry anyone. Not tonight. Day after tomorrow would be soon enough. Her mother would be back by then. She'd ask her mother.

––––––––––

Holden was frustrated at the holdup in traffic. "New Year's Eve," he muttered to himself. Glancing at his watch, he knew he wouldn't get to Mattie's before ten-thirty. *I should have started sooner,* he thought,

although it was good to know the last of the downtown project was finished. All that remained was the
bookwork. He patted the briefcase on the seat beside
him. He could work on that in Summerwind next
week. Then he could begin to think about his own
life, and his life with Karissa and the baby. *I wonder
if she'll agree,* he thought. *If we married before the
baby came, I could be listed as the father. Or at least
the baby would have Kelley for a last name.*

Holden checked his rearview mirror. Traffic as far
back as he could see was stopped dead in its tracks,
and he couldn't tell how far ahead it was held up, either. He fumbled with the radio dial, hoping to catch
the news or a traffic report. Stuck between hills, the
radio spat nothing but static. He began to thump his
thumbs on the steering wheel. It was a good thing
Karissa didn't know he was coming. No need to worry
her.

———

Mattie checked the clock. Nearly nine. Holden
should be pulling in any minute. "I don't think I can
keep her up more than another half hour," she told
Ben. "Look at her, she's so sleepy she can hardly hold
her head up."

"Let her go to bed," Ben said. "We can get her up
when Holden gets here. She doesn't know he's coming anyway. Why torture the poor thing?"

Mattie crossed the room and came into the living
room, where Karissa was dozing on the sofa. Tenderly
touching her forehead, Mattie whispered, "Karissa?
Why don't you go on up to bed. It's almost nine."

"Nine? I thought Holden would call by now."

"Ben and I'll stay up a little while. If he calls I'll tell
him you were too tired to wait any longer. He'll understand, dear."

"But I don't want to miss his call."

"I know, Kassy. But look at you, you're bushed. You don't have the energy to keep your head up. Go on, dear. I'll tell him. You can talk to him in the morning."

Karissa moved awkwardly to the stairway and climbed slowly to her room. She rubbed her aching back and looked forward to slipping between the clean sheets she and Mattie had put on earlier in the day.

Kate had warned her that she'd be uncomfortable the last few weeks, but Karissa couldn't have imagined it would be this uncomfortable. She placed her hands on her swollen middle. Sometimes it felt soft, other times it tensed as hard as an overinflated basketball. She poked her tummy with her finger. It was as hard as a watermelon. Between the spasms high in her inner thighs and the aching in her back, she didn't take time to read her Bible as she had in the past. She got into bed and slipped gratefully to sleep.

---

Holden was fit to be tied. Traffic was beginning to creep at two miles per hour. He couldn't tell if it was really moving, or if people were just closing every spare inch between their cars.

"What's going on up there, man?" Holden rolled down his window to speak to the stranger walking down the narrow shoulder.

"Bad one, I'm afraid." The man approached Holden's open window. "Four or five cars so mangled together we can't tell. Bodies lying all over the pavement. Blood everywhere." He scanned the distance. "The ambulance is having trouble getting in because people have jammed the shoulder trying to make another traffic lane." The man shook his head. "Not a pretty sight."

"Need some help?"

"Could use some strong backs up there. We're try-ing to get a woman out now. If we could get her out, maybe we could move the cars over to the side and get some of this traffic moving."

Without hesitation Holden bolted from his car and sprinted toward the accident scene. Flashing lights surrounded the area and an ambulance was finally arriving.

"Over here!" someone shouted as he approached. "Give us a hand, will you? Take the front, there. See if you can see anything, okay? We'll pull from back here."

Together the impromptu army of rescue workers found a way to pull the meshed cars apart. Muscles rippled and steel gave way. Holden caught sight of a young woman about Karissa's age trapped beneath the dashboard. "Hold it!" he shouted. "There's a woman in here!"

Holden leaned in as far as he could and felt around to see if anything was penetrating the young woman's body. Fairly certain that she wouldn't be hurt worse by being released, he signaled to the men waiting for the word. "All right, when I say 'now' you pull like crazy! I'll try to get her out of here."

Carefully, he slid his strong hands under the woman and saw her open her eyes slightly. "Don't worry, we'll get you out of here." He thought he saw the flicker of a smile before her face grimaced in pain.

"Okay—NOW!" Holden yelled at the top of his lungs. The cars moved only inches, but it was enough for Holden to free her trapped arm. Once he got her arm tucked across her rib cage, he felt around for her feet. He knew he didn't have much time. He was afraid that one of her feet may be caught but knew if the men let go of the car they could crush her to death. He breathed a quick prayer and swiftly lifted her from the wreckage.

Carrying her over to the shoulder of the road, he laid her carefully on an assortment of jackets and coats that appeared out of nowhere. She coughed and moaned as Holden tried to let go of her head. She opened her eyes and Holden knew she was trying to say something. Bending over, he heard her whisper, "Please . . . hold . . . me."

"I don't want to hurt you, miss."

"Hold . . . me . . ."

Holden sat beside her and cradled her head next to his chest. He looked into her pain-filled eyes and for a moment saw Julie. His heart gripped with the pain of what his precious young wife had experienced.

"Thank . . . you . . . I didn't want . . . to . . . die . . . alone . . . in . . . there."

Holden smiled at her, and she closed her eyes and whispered, "Jesus, Jesus . . ." He felt her whole body go limp. He carefully stroked her face for several minutes before he realized—she was dead.

Sitting quietly, he let the tears fall freely and splash across the lifeless young face. He rocked her gently and smoothed her dark hair away from her bruised face. He held her for several minutes until a highway patrolman came and tapped him on the shoulder. "She's gone, son."

"I know," Holden said simply. "I know."

Several strong arms lifted the lifeless burden from Holden's arms. He turned and crawled to the edge of the highway and let the deep, soul-wrenching sobs surface. He lay on his stomach in the dirt and knew he was going to be sick.

"Hey man, you okay?" The stranger who had enlisted his help earlier slapped him lightly on the back.

Holden wiped his face on his sleeve. "I'll be okay."

"They're about ready to move traffic. You better

get back to your truck. You okay to drive? We don't want another scene like this tonight."

"Or ever," Holden said. "I'll be fine."

*God, oh, God,* Holden prayed silently once traffic began to move. One of his deepest inner struggles concerning Julie's death was that she had died in someone else's arms. He had always felt guilty that he wasn't with her, yet indebted to the man who had shared that moment with her down in the ravine. He couldn't help but feel a deep sense that tonight that debt had been repaid.

*Inasmuch as ye have done it unto one of the least of these,* the Bible said, *ye have done it unto me.* Holden was glad he hadn't hesitated to be with the dying young woman. In a way he felt a strange sense of healing by the experience of her death. To be with someone that close to their death was almost like witnessing the very moment of birth. Eternity was so close—only a narrow threshold either side of birth or death.

The presence of the Lord seemed so real Holden was tempted to reach out and touch it. He was anxious to be near Karissa, to tell her of his plan. Tonight's experience convinced him even more. Conventional or not, he wanted to be married as soon as possible.

# Twenty-eight

Karissa stirred in her sleep. Even without her knowing, she was uncomfortable. The minute she felt the wetness, she bolted awake. Bounding from the bed, she ran to the small bathroom, leaving a wet trail across the room.

Cleaning herself up as well as she could, she called for Mattie.

"What is it, dear?" Mattie stood at the bottom of the stairs. Karissa couldn't believe that Mattie could sound so awake and close by in the middle of the night.

"Mattie! I think my water broke!"

"You think? Don't you know for sure?"

"Mattie! Oh, Mattie!"

Mattie walked calmly up the stairway and cautiously opened the bathroom door. Karissa's eyes were wide and her cheeks flushed with excitement.

"What's happening?"

"I was sleeping, I don't know—suddenly there was a gush. I'm afraid I've left a mess behind me."

"Don't you worry about that one bit."

"Yikes!"

"What's the matter?"

"I'm having terrible cramping. Mattie, do you think I'm in labor?"

"That's very likely. I think we'd better figure out how we're going to get you to the hospital. Can you get yourself back to the bed while I go down and call the doctor?"

"I think so." Karissa grabbed a towel and stuck it between her legs. Carefully, she walked toward the bed, but only made it to a chair before another contraction sent her almost to her knees. She leaned forward and gingerly sat on the chair.

"How can I reach your mother?" Mattie called from below.

"I don't know. What time is it?"

"Just before ten."

"It's only ten?" Karissa had only been asleep an hour. "They were all going to church at nine-thirty." Karissa knew her parents would be repeating their vows before another hour passed. "Mattie, can't we call Mark? I don't want my parents to miss their own wedding vows!"

"Let's see, he was going to the country club tonight, wasn't he?"

"Hurry, Mattie!"

"Hang on, dear. I'm calling him now." Mattie flipped through the phone book and dialed the number. "Mark Andrews, please. Emergency." Karissa heard Mattie shout into the phone. "Yes, it's an emergency!" Then a pause. "They're paging him, Karissa."

Karissa reached for her robe and slippers. She felt the pressure ease in her lower abdomen and decided to try to dress in something comfortable. Standing, she felt all right and almost called to Mattie to tell Mark not to hurry after all when another spasm doubled her over. She let out a moan and heard Mattie's voice again.

"Thank goodness you're here. She's upstairs."

"What's the matter?"

*Holden! Holden is here!*

"She's in labor. I'm calling Mark."

"Tell him to meet us at the hospital. He'd better go get her parents."

"No!" Karissa yelled. "They're about to say their

vows. Let them come afterward."

Holden took the stairs two at a time. He burst into Karissa's bedroom. The sight of her crowded out the ugliness of the horrid accident scene he had left just hours ago. While death had been sprawled all over the highway, a new life was about to be born in this very room unless he could get Karissa to the hospital in time. In spite of himself, Holden laughed softly at her appearance. Sitting on the chair, her cotton robe and gown were stretched tightly across her bulging stomach, and her long blond hair, normally so well-groomed, fell in tangles across her bright pink cheeks.

Karissa felt a stab of embarrassment at Holden's seeing her like this, but before she could protest, another pain hit. Unable to speak, she held her hand up and bit her lower lip to keep from crying out. Finally, as the pain subsided, she took a deep breath in and exhaled slowly.

"Okay, can we make it downstairs before the next one hits?" Holden asked.

"I hope so." Karissa reached for a blanket and demanded a clean towel from the bathroom cabinet.

"A towel? We've come that far already?" Holden asked.

"I hope you're not fussy about your seat covers," Karissa said.

"Not at all. I'm in the truck."

"Oh, great."

"We can take your car," Holden said.

"I don't think I can squeeze into it anymore."

"You want to ride in the back of the pickup?" Holden was determined to be lighthearted as he helped Karissa through this. He had been able to do nothing for the young woman who lay dying in his arms earlier, but this young woman about to give birth needed him to put it behind him, out of his mind, and be strong and cheerful for her.

"Don't you wish."

"Let's go."

Effortlessly, Holden swooped her up in his arms and carried her down the stairs. Ben sat staring at the New Year's Eve celebration on TV.

"Guy Lombardo has announced the New Year in New York. You'd better hurry if you're going to have that baby this year," he said pointing at the TV.

"Men!" Mattie scolded. "What's the matter with the two of you? This girl's got a long night ahead of her. Don't be rushing her now."

"What about Mark?" Holden asked as he kicked open the back door.

"He said he'd meet you there."

"Oh, great," Karissa said. "I'll have the two of you pacing in the father's room."

"He's going by River Place Community to leave a message for your folks. He said he'd make sure they didn't get it until after their little ceremony."

Mattie helped Holden tuck Karissa into the truck. As he came around and got in, Karissa noticed the blood stains on his shirt.

"Holden! What's that?"

"I'll tell you later. Right now, baby, you've got enough to think about just getting that new little person born."

The next contraction took Karissa's breath away and her mind off anything other than the task at hand.

———

"You the husband?" the brusque woman behind the window asked.

"Well, no," Holden said.

"Where's the husband?"

"He's not coming."

"And why not?" the woman demanded.

"He's dead."

"Oh," she said quietly. "I see."

"Who are you?"

"The boyfriend." Holden couldn't remember when he'd had more fun. He watched the stout woman hike her shoulders and lift her chin.

"Well," she said. "This is highly improper. Only husbands are allowed in the labor room. You'll have to wait out here."

"Not on your life," Holden challenged.

"Out here." The woman was more than definite.

"But she'll be all alone," Holden whined.

"Hardly," the woman said. "The nurses will be with her. Just wait here. We'll let you know when anything happens."

Holden watched helplessly as Karissa was wheeled away from him. He could hardly stand being separated from her any time; now it was unbearable. Then he did what was expected of him—the only thing he could do—he paced.

"Where is she?" Kate's face was white. Gerry followed immediately behind her.

"She's in the labor room. If you get in at all, you'll have to go through the border guard." Holden nodded toward the woman behind the window.

"Are you her mother?" the woman asked when Kate inquired.

"Yes." Kate brushed back a lock of the same blond hair that covered Karissa's head.

"In here, then. The men will have to wait out here."

"Mama?" Karissa's voice sounded faint and tired.

"How're you doing?"

"It's hard work, isn't it?"

Kate laughed. "That's why they call it labor." She

inspected the blankets and patted Karissa's cheek. "They give you anything?"

"Not yet." Karissa's face scrunched up at the next pain.

"Breathe, Kassy, breathe." Kate reached for Karissa's hand. "Squeeze, honey, squeeze my hand."

Mother and daughter shared the experience together. Experience held priority over profession, and the nurses soon realized Kate knew as much about this as they did.

"The doctor's on his way; we're taking her to the delivery room now. You can wait here, or you can join the men." Kate watched as Karissa was carted into the delivery room.

"I want to be as near to her as I can," Kate said. "Can I wait by the delivery room?"

"How many times you been through this?"

"Six," Kate said. "But this is the first time as a grandmother."

"How about standing over here?"

Kate recognized the large black woman who spoke to her.

"You can see in the window. We don't usually let anyone this close, but lands' sake, woman! You're a good customer of ours. We'll make an exception in your case."

"Thanks," Kate smiled at the nurse.

"I almost didn't recognize you, standing on your feet with your clothes on." The broad white smile seemed to fill the whole room. "How long's it been?"

"Two years."

"When's the next one?"

"That's the end of it, I hope. Grandbaby time now." Kate turned her attention to Karissa. "Push, Kassy, push," she whispered.

"You'll have to do better than that if she's gonna hear you," the nurse said. "Go on, nobody knows better than a grandmama how that baby's gonna come on outa there."

"Push! Kassy, push!" Kate yelled. "Wait, honey, rest." Kate watched the doctor and caught his eye as he nodded toward her.

"Again!" the doctor shouted.

"Now, Kassy! Push!" Kate could almost feel Karissa's pain. "Don't give up, push!" She watched her daughter curl up and the team of nurses around her cheering her on. She watched the doctor move back quickly and hold up a squalling messy baby . . . girl!

"It's a girl!" Kate screamed at the familiar black face standing at her elbow. Immediately, she flung herself into the outstretched, generous arms.

"Congratulations, Grandmama. You got yourself a fine-lookin' granddaughter there. Look at all that hair! She's a might tiny, but that voice of hers certainly tells us she was ready to make her way into this world. Blessed Jesus, would you look at that?"

"You said that after the birth of the last two of mine," Kate said.

"It's my way of callin' the good Lord's attention to them right off," the nurse said.

"Thank you," Kate said, "but He's been aware of this one for quite a while. I've made sure of that."

"I bet you have, missus. A little miracle every time." The nurse dabbed at the tears flowing from her eyes. "I never get over it. Well, now, you going to go tell that group of anxious men out there, or shall I?"

"I'll go," Kate said. "But I'll be right back."

"Go get that new daddy and bring him back in here."

"Well, that would be kind of difficult. You see, he's . . ." Kate paused, then her face broke into a wide smile. "I'll see what I can do."

"Jus' tell him to look for me."

Kate watched the nurse put both hands on her wide hips.

"Don' settle for anyone else, you hear?"

"Perfectly." Kate walked toward the room where Holden was waiting.

# Twenty-nine

"What's going on?" Phyllis was slightly drunk. "I had to get Roberta and Seth Martin to drive me over here. You left without telling me."

Mark took his wife by the elbow and walked her toward the exit. Nodding at the Martins, he led them away from Holden and Gerry just as Kate was coming down the hall.

"It's Karissa, she's in labor," Mark said. "She'll probably have the baby tonight." Mark glanced across the room at Holden's face as it broke into a broad smile. Kate gathered the young man in her arms and Holden nodded toward Mark. He wanted to rejoin the small family group, but he wanted to make sure Phyllis wasn't going to spoil their moment. He quickly ushered her outside in the cool night air.

"Listen to me, Phyllis," Mark warned. "You're not going to make a spectacle of yourself in there." Roberta and Seth moved away and Mark nodded his thanks. "You've been drinking and I'm not going to let you ruin this for them. You hear me?"

"Get off your high horse, Mark." Phyllis's speech was slightly slurred. "Michael's baby is about to make his entrance. I'm his grandmother. I have as much right to be here as anyone. In fact, maybe more."

"What do you mean by that?"

"Just this, Mr. Righteous, I talked to a lawyer at the party tonight. That's right, a lawyer. He says I have a right to that baby."

Mark's heart stopped beating for a moment, then pounded to life again. "What?"

"Just you watch," she stepped sideways, almost tripped, and regained her balance before Mark caught her arm in his tight grip. "I'll sue for custody if I have to. I've already caught Karissa with two men—it wouldn't be difficult to prove my case."

"You're drunk."

"Maybe a little. But I'm sober enough to know exactly what I'm talking about."

"Then listen to this, Phyllis. I have also seen a lawyer. I have divorce papers all drawn up and ready to serve. You make one false step toward that baby or Karissa, and I swear I'll divorce you. With the reports from my auditors and the bank records, I have everything I need to cut you off without a cent."

"You won't do that, Mark. I know you won't."

"Oh, won't I?"

"I'll sue you for every penny you have. I'll take it all."

"You already have, Phyllis, I have nothing else to lose."

"I'll take the business."

"The business is broke."

"I'll take the house."

"You can have it."

"I'll take the cars."

"Fine."

"I'll take the rest of the property up on the east end."

"No, you won't. I sold it last week and the money is already in trust for the baby." Mark stepped away from his wife. "Face it, Phyllis, you've lost it all. Michael, me—everything. It's gone."

"I will get that baby," she said meekly.

"No, you won't." Mark stood his ground. He had

let her manage and ruin Michael; he wasn't about to let her near the baby.

Mark glanced back to where Karissa's parents and Holden stood. He watched as Kate gently nudged Holden toward the hallway and then turned back into her husband's embrace.

"Go home, Phyllis. Go back to the club. Go anywhere but here. You don't belong here." Mark watched his wife stagger toward the curb.

———

Holden made his way toward the small labor room where Karissa had been taken for a few moments alone with her new daughter. He was joined in the outer hallway by the large black woman in white who stepped in front of him.

"'Scuse us, please. Let the new papa through." Her flashing white teeth sparkled above a soft row of double chins. No one argued or questioned her authority or Holden's presence.

"But, I'm not really the—"

"Don't tell me nothin'. I don't want to know anythin'. Here, put this on." She tossed a surgical gown over her shoulder and it landed squarely in Holden's midsection. "You look a mess."

At the doorway, Holden paused and fought back the tears at the sight of Karissa's long blond hair feathered out over her pillow and cascading across her shoulders.

He had stepped quietly to the side of the bed and stood there for a moment before Karissa was aware of him.

"Oh, Holden, look at her. Isn't she beautiful?" Karissa's tears fell onto the top of the downy-soft, honey-colored curls that encircled the little head. She cradled her newborn closely and unwrapped the pink blanket just enough to free one of the baby's tiny fists.

Holden reached toward the baby, and Karissa looked into his deep-set blue eyes. She saw that he, too, was crying, and she immediately pushed the little bundle toward him.

"Go ahead, hold her. You might as well get acquainted."

"You think it'd be okay?"

"Go ahead."

Holden lifted the child, supporting her little body easily with both hands. He slid her into the crook of his arm and instinctively touched her tiny forehead with his kiss.

"Oh, Karissa, she's beautiful." Holden's stomach tightened with emotion. He was totally spent. The night had been the most unusual and unexpected experience of his entire life. Suddenly life and death seemed so natural, only a breath apart. "What's her name?"

"Hope." Karissa smiled. "Hope Kathleen."

"I like that." Holden nodded his approval. "You're no bigger than a little bug, Miss Hope Kathleen," he said to the baby in his arms. "A little katydid bug. Can I call you my little katydid?" Looking at Karissa, he asked, "Can I call her Katie? Do you mind?"

"You can call her anything you like," Karissa whispered. "Besides, my mother would love that."

"Can I call her my daughter?" Holden carefully put Katie back into the arms of her mother before he looked again into Karissa's eyes.

"What?"

"Karissa, will you marry me?"

"Are you sure?"

"Well, I waited to see the baby first. I didn't want an ugly kid," Holden teased. "But now that I see her, yeah, I want to get married. I want us to be a family."

Holden bent close to Karissa's face. She raised her eyes from the face of her child to meet his. "I love you, Holden Kelley," she whispered. "I—we'd like that very much."

"Katie Kelley—sounds like a movie star, doesn't it?" Holden knelt beside the hospital bed and put his head on the pillow next to Karissa's.

"Oh no, Katie, your daddy's making big plans for you already."

Right outside the doorway to the small hospital room, two large, soft hands were clasped close to the ample bosom of Nurse Watkins. "Dear Jesus, you didn't waste any time answerin' that one, now, did you? Bless your precious, holy Name for sure."

# Epilogue

On Easter afternoon, Karissa and Holden stood facing Jim Henry between large baskets of lush ferns and Easter lilies in the high-school-gymnasium-turned-church. Mark sat beside Kate and Gerry on the front row, holding three-month-old Katie.

"Where's Phyllis?" Gerry whispered to Mark. "We thought she'd be here."

"Vegas." Mark glanced momentarily at Gerry, then back to Karissa and Holden.

" . . . I now pronounce you man and wife. Holden, you may kiss your bride."

Holden turned to smile at Karissa. She wore a pink linen suit and her long blond hair tumbled from her matching pillbox hat in waves and soft curls to the middle of her back. Holden pulled her close and just before he covered her lips with his own, he whispered, "I love you, Kassy."

Kate dabbed a tear from her eye, and Gerry pulled out his handkerchief and blew his nose.

"Before I introduce the new couple," Pastor Jim said as Holden lifted his lips from Karissa's, "they have asked to present their daughter, Hope Kathleen, to the Lord in dedication as their first act as husband and wife. If the grandparents would join us, please."

Mark handed Katie to Holden and they all stood to face Jim together.

"As the parents of our Lord and Savior Jesus Christ brought Him to the temple to be presented before the Lord, we also now present this little one. This dedication is not just of the baby, but this is the time when Holden and Karissa dedicate themselves as parents. Realizing they have been entrusted with the care of this little child, they recognize their responsibility, accept it, and pledge before the Father, Son, and Holy Spirit to the best of their abilities to model on a daily basis the life of Christ to this precious little girl. Holden, Karissa, is that your pledge?"

"It is," they said in unison.

"Do you pledge to teach her what it means to accept Christ as her own personal Savior as an act of her own free will?"

"We do," Holden and Karissa said.

"Let us pray." Jim took Katie in his arms and raised his face as he prayed.

"Dear Heavenly Father, it is by your miraculous grace that you have joined Holden and Karissa this day, not only as husband and wife, but as the committed parents of Hope Kathleen. It is by their pledge that I present them to you, our God, as they dedicate their marriage and this child to you. In Christ, in whose name we pray."

Jim Henry kissed wide-eyed Katie and held her so those attending could see her bright little face framed by the fluffy eyelet bonnet. Handing her to Kate, he said, "And, grandparents, do you also pledge to model the life of Christ as it's lived out through His children to this child?"

"We do," Mark, Gerry, and Kate said together.

"Mark, please hold Hope Kathleen, will you?"

"Mark Andrews, do you also pledge, as little Katie's godfather, to have always as your priority her well-being, and will you take full responsibility for her spiritual upbringing should Holden or Karissa fail or be unable to do so?"

"Gladly." Mark smiled down at his granddaughter. Kissing her, he then handed her back to Holden.

"Now, finally," Jim smiled, "it is my special privilege to present to you Mr. and Mrs. Holden Kelley—and family."

# Non-fiction Books by Neva Coyle

Abiding Study Guide
Daily Thoughts on Living Free
Diligence Study Guide
Discipline tape album (4 cassettes)
Free to Be Thin, The All-New (with Marie Chapian)
Free to Be Thin Lifestyle Plan, The All-New
Free to Be Thin Cookbook
Free to Be Thin Daily Planner
Free to Dream
Freedom Study Guide
Learning to Know God
Living by Chance or by Choice
Living Free
Living Free Seminar Study Guide
Making Sense of Pain and Struggle
Meeting the Challenges of Change
A New Heart . . . A New Start
Obedience Study Guide
Overcoming the Dieting Dilemma
Perseverance Study Guide
Restoration Study Guide
Slimming Down and Growing Up (with Marie Chapian)
There's More to Being Thin Than Being Thin (with Marie
    Chapian)